I was looking for one with an angel code on it. Molly was looking for one with Celtic markings. We weren't getting very far. The fog just kept getting thicker and thicker, and we were chilled to our bones.

"Maybe we should find shelter," Molly said.

"Okay," I agreed. We turned our backs to the wind and walked backward, trying to avoid bumping into the headstones. If we could get inside the old church walls again, at least they would break the wind a bit.

Just then, for a split second, the wind cleared the fog away where my torch was pointed. It shone on a grave with a new headstone on it.

I directed the torch slowly up and down the headstone. "Molly!" I whispered, reaching for her arm. My voice barely came out. My knees felt weak. What we saw made us both scream.

Hannah and the Angels
Saving Uncle Seán

by Linda Lowery Keep

Based on a concept by
Linda Lowery Keep
and Carole Newhouse

Random House New York

Cover art © 1999 by Peter Van Ryzin

Copyright © 1999 by Renegade Angel, Inc., and
Newhouse/Haft Associates, Inc.
HANNAH AND THE ANGELS is a trademark of Random House, Inc.,
Renegade Angel, Inc., and Newhouse/Haft Associates, Inc.
RANDOM HOUSE and colophon are registered
trademarks of Random House, Inc.
All rights reserved under International and Pan-American Copyright
Conventions. Published in the United States by Random House, Inc.,
New York, and simultaneously in Canada by Random House of
Canada Limited, Toronto.

www.randomhouse.com/kids

Library of Congress Cataloging-in-Publication Data
Keep, Linda Lowery.
Hannah and the angels: Saving Uncle Seán/by Linda Lowery Keep.
SUMMARY: Her angels transport eleven-year-old Hannah to Ireland, where
her special mission is to solve a mystery involving an old monastery, a
freshly dug grave, and missing money.
ISBN: 0-375-80095-6
[1. Angels—Fiction. 2. Space and time—Fiction. 3. Ireland—Fiction.
4. Mystery and detective stories.] I. Title. II. Series: Keep, Linda Lowery.
Hannah and the angels; bk. #5   PZ7.K25115Sav 1999
[Fic]—dc21   99-21400

Printed in the United States of America
10 9 8 7 6 5 4 3 2 1

For my grandaunt Bea from Aughrim, Ireland,
and all her grandangels

Acknowledgments

My thanks to all those who "traveled" with Hannah and me to Ireland, especially:

My wonderful editor, Lisa Banim, who has a special knack for Irish English.

My cousin Triona Ryan, who teaches at Schoil Mhuire Naofa in County Meath, for her enormous help with Molly's Gaelic, the standing-stone Ogham message, and Hannah's adventures in Aran.

The authors of all the research materials I used, particularly Eamonn Brennan and Liam Hernon, whose book *Ages Ago* was a great help with the Celtic arts and the Ogham stones.

Eileen Lucas, for always reminding me that whenever a door closes, another opens.

And for all my family who stayed rooted in Ireland while their sisters and brothers and aunts and uncles sailed for North America years ago: the Hessions, Lowerys, Shanahans, Hogans, and Salmons, and especially Kevin, Ann, and Mary Ryan of Aughrim, County Galway.

Contents

Hannah and the Angels
Saving Uncle Seán

Chapter 1

The Gift of Gab

I, Hannah Martin, have the gift of gab. I always have something to say. Well, hey, life is interesting, you know what I mean? So why not talk about it? But some people think I talk a little *too* much. My friend David, for instance. He says the gift of gab is also called blarney, and that I probably get it from the Irish side of my family. That's my dad's side.

"I don't want words, I want *action*," David says.

He's referring to the whole stupid thing about his queen. Okay, so I gave away his precious queen chess piece a long time ago (well, not *that* long ago), when I was on my angel trip to Africa. And I meant to replace it. I really did. It's just that I haven't had a chance yet.

"Pleeeease, David," I begged the other day. "Let's play a game of chess."

David and I were supposed to be writing our homework poems about the Nobel Peace Prize that two Irish men had won. I could not get my poem to rhyme, and I was getting frustrated. I needed a break.

"Just one game?" I pleaded.

"Return my queen and I'll think about it," said David. He didn't look up from his poem. He was still mad at me.

I tried my best to talk my way around it. "I've been soooo busy with school, and chores at home, and trying to figure out ways to wear my hair now that I'm growing it long." (Not to mention my angel missions!)

"Excuses, excuses," said David, quietly continuing to work on his poem. But I had an idea.

"Here, this will work for now," I said, picking up a blue plastic troll with hot pink hair. It belonged to David's twin sister, Katie, my other best friend.

"A *troll* for a queen?" said David. "Are you out of your mind?"

"What's wrong with her?" I said. "She's perfect. Her feet fit right into that little black square."

David picked up the troll by its fuzzy hair and dangled it as if it had cooties. "This is like inviting an alien into the chess

Troll Queen

game. No, Hannah. I want my queen back."

"Picky, picky, picky," I complained, setting up the game anyway. "What's the big deal?" I reached for my flute case, pretending to ignore anything David had to say.

"The big deal is that it's a chess *set*," David explained. "Get it? The pieces all match, like a royal family."

I moved my pawn. "Come on, David," I said stubbornly. "It's your move."

He crossed his arms. "Forget it, Hannah. You just don't get it."

I got it, all right. David was being a jerk.

But I wouldn't give up. I never do. "What's the matter?" I asked. "Can't you win a game with a blue alien troll queen? You think she's a jinx?" I fitted the pieces of my flute together and tooted a few irritating notes.

David grabbed the troll and tossed it toward Katie's wastebasket.

"Hey!" Katie yelled, catching the troll as she walked in. "What's with you two? I thought you were writing about peace!"

"We were, until David decided to be a jerk," I said, really ticked off now.

"I am not a jerk," said David.

"Are too," I said.

"Am not!" he shot back.

"You guys are both acting like babies," said Katie, sounding disgusted. "I'm going to mediate

here, just like we did in Ms. Montgomery's class."
Ms. Montgomery's our substitute teacher. She gets
hyper about settling problems without fighting.

I groaned. Between the peace poem and all
that conflict-resolution stuff Ms. Montgomery put
us through at school all day, I'd already had
enough. I just wanted to play chess.

Katie stood on her head and
twisted into her thinking position,
wrapping her legs into a pretzel.
She actually believes she thinks
better that way.

"We can try to get you
guys to quit fighting in several different ways," she said,

Katie's mediator viewpoint

from upside down. "You could count to ten and
cool off…"

David and I both rolled our eyes to the ceiling.

"But I think we should start by taking turns
speaking and listening to each other," Katie went
on. She never gives up.

"I'll go first," I volunteered. "I have a very
good point to make here."

With that, David put on his earphones and
started head-bobbing to the music.

"And David has a good point, too," Katie said
to me. "Maybe this time you could let *him* go
first."

I turned my chair away from David. "What
good point?" I complained. "That he'll never for-

give me for not replacing his dumb queen?" Obviously I'm not as good at listening as I am at gabbing. But I guess you've figured that out already.

Katie kept talking in her calm mediator voice, and I kept not listening. I started playing my flute again.

"Go ahead, David," Katie was saying. "It's your turn first…"

As I focused on my music, I realized I was playing a tune I'd never even heard. I listened harder. A windy, faraway sound was echoing through the flute. This had happened before. I knew at that very moment it was my angel Lyra. She was going to send me on a new mission!

No matter how many times this happens, I'm amazed every single time, all over again. Me, Hannah Martin, going on another angel mission! Where was I going? Who would I meet there?

I still can't believe I have *four* angels: Demetriel, Aurora, Lorielle, and Lyra. And I still can't believe I'm the person they choose to send on secret missions to help people all over the world.

Anyway, I kept tooting my flute. Then I began to feel very light, as if I could fly. I heard the flute hit a faint, high-pitched note, traveling across miles and miles and miles. And then a man's voice said, very quietly and very seriously: "*Peace*."

Chapter 2

Blackbirds at a Burial

"May she rest in peace," another voice said. It was a woman this time.

Where was I? I wasn't playing my flute, mad at David. I wasn't even with him and Katie anymore. I was standing on a hill in some very green grass, under a tree full of noisy blackbirds, getting rained on. My flute had changed into something else. It was light and small, and vertical, like a recorder.

I could see four people, leaning over a deep hole in the ground. Three were dressed all in black—black coats, black shoes, black umbrellas. They looked just like the blackbirds gathered above me.

"May she rest in peace," a

The three blackbirds

second man said. The blackbird people seemed to be taking turns reciting that. One by one, they scooped up handfuls of dirt and threw it in the hole. Now I caught on. It was a grave. Somebody had died!

I felt like maybe I shouldn't be watching. I scooted behind the tree, and as I did, one of the men looked up. Now that I could really see him, I realized he wasn't dressed in crow black like the others. He was wearing regular working clothes— a jacket, a sweater, a cap. I think he saw me. But he quickly turned back to finish the burial. The other two people hugged each other somberly and started to walk away. I watched them closely. Maybe they had something to do with my mission. The man with the cap looked over his shoulder, straight at me. He'd seen me, for sure! Was that good or bad? I had no idea.

When they were all out of sight, I came out from behind the tree.

"You're *her!*" whispered a voice in my ear. I spun around. A girl about my age was standing right behind me, holding an umbrella. She had bright green eyes and light gold hair.

"You're the angel, aren't you?" she said excitedly.

Right away, I knew I was in Ireland. I recognized this girl's Irish brogue. She talked quickly, and her words clicked along, rolling up and down like the green hills.

"No, I'm Hannah Martin," I answered. "Who are you?"

"It's me, Molly Ryan," she said. "I'm so glad they sent you!"

"So glad *who* sent me?"

"Whoever is in charge of the angels!" she said brightly. "I've never met a real angel before! Do you mind if I touch you?" She reached out her hand.

I backed away quickly.

"I'm not an angel," I told her. Yes, angels had sent me. Molly was right on that count. But I think she was a little confused.

Molly gingerly reached out her fingers again and poked my hand, my arm, my shoulder. "I thought you'd feel different. More like a fairy," she said, frowning. "But you feel...human."

"I think you're a little, uh, mixed up," I said. "I *am* human."

Molly burst out laughing. "Don't be silly. I saw you appear out of thin air just a minute ago," she said. "Of course you're an angel, Hannah. The one I talked to last night before I went to sleep!"

Since Molly had actually seen me appear out of nowhere, I was going to have to be honest.

"My angels sent me here," I admitted. "I'm from Wisconsin."

Molly looked surprised. "You're not from heaven, then?" she asked.

Oh no! This girl was determined to think I was an angel. I had a feeling this would take some major explaining. I tried to change the subject.

"So who died?" I asked.

To my surprise, a man's voice answered. "The dearly departed," he said, "was a Mrs. Nora Lynch."

Molly and I jumped three feet. There, right behind us, was the guy in the cap who'd been watching me from the grave. He must have hiked up the other side of the hill. His sweater and jacket looked pretty dirty up close.

"Hello, Mr. Sullivan," said Molly. "You startled us."

"I didn't mean to do that," he said. "Sorry now."

"I didn't know Nora Lynch," Molly went on. "She wasn't from around here, was she?"

"No," said Mr. Sullivan. "She lived in Aran."

"Ah, the Aran Islands?" asked Molly.

"Yes," he said, nodding sadly. "But she wanted to be laid to rest in a beautiful green place. Her family brought her here."

"Her family buried her in a place where nobody knows her?" Molly asked, sounding surprised.

"Ay," said Mr. Sullivan. "'Tis a pity she won't be resting near her kin. But they say it's what she wanted, so who was I to say she couldn't be buried here?"

The drizzle was falling harder and colder now.

"Well, it's time I should be getting back to my work," said Mr. Sullivan. "My best to all your family, Molly Ryan." He walked off, down the hill, to the grave. No one was there now. Even the blackbirds had flown away. Mr. Sullivan picked up a shovel and began filling the grave with clumps of wet dirt.

"Is he the gravedigger?" I asked. That would explain why he was so dirty.

Molly gave me a shocked look. "I thought angels knew everything," she said.

"I'm *not* an angel!" I said for what seemed like the tenth time. "I'm a regular girl from Wisconsin. In the United States."

The gravedigger

Molly winked. "Don't worry, Angel Hannah," she said. "I won't tell a soul."

I groaned. There was no changing this girl's mind.

"Anyway, yes. Mr. Sullivan is the gravedigger," Molly explained. "He'll be filling up the hole with earth. Then, in a few days, he'll fit a proper headstone for poor Nora Lynch, rest her soul."

Suddenly a frown darkened Molly's bright face. She linked her arm through mine and guided me down the back side of the soggy hill.

"Now let's get down to the matter at hand, Angel Hannah," she said. She sounded troubled. "Something terrible has happened, and you're the only one who can fix it."

Chapter 3

Trouble in Emerald City

I ducked under Molly's umbrella and followed her down the hill, through the green grass, and along the river. Green, green, green. Everything around me was green. Even the fog and the gray stone fences had pale tints of green. The only thing that wasn't green was the sheep. They were fluffy white.

"It's like being in the Emerald City of Oz!" I told Molly.

"'Tis," she agreed. "Sure, don't we call it the Emerald Isle?"

Molly told me about the Celtic Arts Centre, which was being built nearby. She's an Irish step dancer (step dancing is a special kind of folk dancing, in shoes with taps on them), and she couldn't wait to have a place where she could meet famous dancers from all over Ireland.

While I was listening to Molly, I couldn't help thinking about leprechauns. You know, those mischievous little men with the beards who blend in with all the green in Ireland and play tricks on you? I wondered if they were real, and if I might actually see one. Anything was possible, I had a feeling, in Ireland.

Molly's family lived in the most wonderful home. It looked like the Three Bears' house, small and white, with a bright blue door. The inside was cozy, and a warm fire was burning.

In the firelight, I noticed for the first time that Molly had a lot of freckles. In fourth grade, Katie and I went through a freckle phase. We wanted freckles so badly, we put pen dots on our noses and cheeks to look cute. The only problem was, we used permanent markers, so we couldn't get the dots off for our fourth-grade class pictures. Our parents were not nearly as delighted about our freckles as we were.

No one seemed to be home. We hung our wet clothes by the fire. I felt like I needed to be wrung out and hung up, too. I smelled all damp and woolly. Molly gave me a heavy cream-colored sweater to wear.

"Do you need to cut holes in the back for your wings, Hannah?" she asked. I couldn't

Me, hanging on the line

tell whether she was teasing me. I had the weird feeling she wasn't.

"I told you, I'm not an angel!" I said. I turned in a circle, to show her that the sweater fit just fine, with no lumps in back where I was trying to hide a pair of wings. "Look, no wings!"

"Tea?" asked Molly, ignoring the wing thing. She hung a heavy black kettle on a hook over the fire.

"Uh, sure," I said. I'm not much of a tea drinker, but if I put in lots of milk and sugar, it's kind of like having cocoa. Molly brought out bread with raisins in it, and butter and jam. We sat on low stools in front of the fire.

"Here's why I've been hoping you'd come," Molly began. She pulled out a piece of paper that was a flyer for some kind of show:

CELTIC ARTS CENTRE

CEILI

DANCERS! MUSICIANS!

SINGERS!

PRIZES!

"What's a see-lee?" I asked. I was trying to pronounce *ceili*.

Molly giggled. "Don't angels speak Irish?" she asked. "It's pronounced KAY-lee. It's a dance. A big party."

"You want me to come to a party?" I asked, bewildered.

"Not exactly," said Molly. "It's more like I want you to *save* a party."

"Tell me what's happened," I said.

Molly's green eyes darkened. "All the money raised for the new arts centre was stolen last night!"

I frowned. Could this be my mission?

"My uncle, Seán Ryan, started raising money for the arts centre two years ago. People from all over the country worked hard to add their donations. We finally had enough to start building."

"And...?" I asked. Yes, this might be the kind of problem my angels would want me to help solve.

"Well, Uncle Seán took the money home last night, planning to deposit it in the bank first thing this morning. He went out to the pub for less than an hour, and when he got back, it was gone!"

Just then, the door swung open, and a brisk wind whipped through the house. Molly's mother and two little brothers had arrived home.

"Oh, Molly, 'tis a terrible, terrible thing that's happened!" cried her mom.

I could see the two boys had been crying.

Their faces were smudged from rubbing their eyes with dirty hands. They hung up their wet coats and came over by the fire with their teacups. The two of them were very cute. One had bright red hair and the other was blond, like Molly. Both of them had freckles.

"What is it, Mum?" asked Molly. Then she remembered me. "Oh, this is my friend Hannah. She's come from America for a holiday. Hannah, this is my mum and Kevin and Jimmy."

The boys turned their puppy eyes to me. The younger one, Jimmy (the redhead), went to stand behind his mom.

"But we didn't expect you, Hannah!" said Mrs. Ryan, looking worried. "'Tis a shame you had to come right now, in the middle of all these troubles."

"That's okay, Mum," said Molly. "Hannah was meant to come here now." She gave me a secret wink. Obviously this girl still believed I was an angel.

I suddenly wished I *could* be an angel. It sure would make everybody feel better if I could just swoop in, find the missing money, lock the thieves behind bars, and fly back out. I knew that wasn't how my angels worked, but still...

I thought I'd give them a try anyway. I turned and stared at the fireplace. "I want to be an angel," I whispered into the flames. "Just for this trip. Please."

Instantly I got a tug on my hair. *Ouch!* It was

Another tug from Demi.

really more like a yank. My guardian angel, Demetriel, was letting me know, in no uncertain terms, that transforming me into an angel, even temporarily, was *not* an option.

"Not in a million millennia!" I heard Demi say. "You do your job, Hannah. We angels will do ours."

I smoothed down my hair. Fine. At least I knew for sure now that my angels were here in Ireland with me. I'd have to convince Molly that we'd have to try to solve Uncle Seán's problem in a down-to-earth way. I turned back to the Ryans' conversation.

"I overheard some talk at the market," Molly's mom was saying. She choked back a sob. "People are whispering that Uncle Seán himself stole the money!"

"No!" cried Molly.

"They're saying why else would Uncle Seán take the money to his own house!" Kevin piped in.

"And they said nobody but Uncle Seán knew it was there!" said Jimmy.

"Who is making these accusations?" Molly demanded, jumping up.

"Everyone," said Mrs. Ryan, dabbing at her eyes. "Gossip can be vicious, you know. Once it gets started…"

"Then somebody tells somebody else," said Kevin.

"And that somebody tells somebody," added Jimmy.

"And soon the truth is twisted and turned inside out, and people start to really believe it," finished Mrs. Ryan.

"We must find the true thief before this gets worse," said Molly.

"Oh, poor Seán!" wailed Mrs. Ryan.

The boys gathered by the fire at their mother's feet, trying to console her.

Molly scooted her stool close to mine. "You can see her heart is breaking," she whispered. "Our family's name will be dishonored. You have to do whatever it is that angels do, and get the money back."

I could see in Molly's pleading eyes that my new friend was counting on me.

How on earth could I convince her I was no angel?

Chapter 4

I'm No Angel (Believe Me!)

Suddenly I had an idea. My backpack! My angels always stash everything in there for me, because you never know what will happen on these trips. If I need something special, there it is! I dumped the contents of my backpack all over the floor in front of the fire. There was a lot of stuff, too. What a mess!

"Look, Molly!" I said. "All these things were packed by my angels."

"Really?" she asked, in awe.

"So if I were an angel myself, I wouldn't need any of this, right?"

Kevin and Jimmy elbowed their way right over, surprised by all the junk. I have to say, I was surprised by some of it, too. I pulled out the little recorder my angels had supplied me with: brass, with a green mouthpiece.

"A penny whistle!" yelled Kevin. "Can I have a go?"

"Sure," I said, handing it over. He immediately started to play a tune. It was the very same one I had been playing when I was in the argument with David, when the angels had started interfering.

"What's that song called?" I asked.

"'Galway Bay,'" said Molly.

I had heard of the name Galway. It's a county in Ireland, but also James Galway is a famous flute player. I try to play like him sometimes, with lots of trills in between the notes. My teacher, Ms. Crybaby (her real name is Ms. Crysler), looks like she's in terrible pain when I do that.

"Is that where we are? Galway?" I asked. Kevin kept right on playing. The music was really, really wonderful. Kevin was, I had to admit, a better player than me. I mean, a better player than *I* (gotcha, Ms. Crybaby!).

"We're not far from there," said Molly. "We're near Galway City, out in the countryside."

Jimmy was eyeballing my Angel Language Decoder. He started spinning the disk around, trying to spell his name.

"Here, let me do that for you," I said. I showed him his name in angel code:

Jimmy

Then I did Kevin's:

𝕐 ☆ ◉ ⁰/₀ ♡

Kevin

"See? My angels send me messages," I told Molly, "and I have to decode them. If I were an angel, I wouldn't need a decoder, right?" She nodded, smiling. Little by little, I think I was convincing her of my *Homo sapiens* status. (That means human, if you didn't guess. *Sapiens* means "wise." David told me that.)

I looked back at the pile on the floor. My trusty journal was with me, as usual. And my rain gear was there—a yellow slicker and rubber boots, which I'd definitely need in this rainy Irish weather. Then I saw something new—a charcoal pencil. And a roll of tape. It wasn't orange, like the tape the angels had sent with me to Mexico for cave exploring. It was plain old masking tape. Pretty boring.

Jimmy opened my box of colored pencils.

"Look at this, Kevin," he was saying. "They're all green."

I frowned. He was right. The colors had changed! No red, no orange, no purple—all green! The names on the side were cool: emerald, lime, and evergreen. Seafoam, kelly, and aquamarine. Shamrock, spring, olive, and mint. Forest, loden, chartreuse, moss, and amazon. That's a lot of green.

"See, Molly? My angels knew I was going to Ireland," I pointed out. "They knew I would need green stuff."

Molly's eyes narrowed. "And just what does that prove?" she asked.

I sighed. "You're right," I said dejectedly. "It doesn't prove a thing."

I wondered if maybe I should tell Molly some of the bad things I'd done in my life. Then she'd know for sure that I wasn't an angel. Like I could tell her about putting hot sauce in Jimmy Fudge's ketchup when he left his french fries sitting on the lunchroom table. On second thought, I decided it wasn't the smartest idea to mention that little episode in front of Kevin and Jimmy. They might get ideas. Did they have hot sauce in Ireland?

I went back to shuffling through my backpack equipment. Wow! I found a camera, the kind that takes instant pictures. I'd always wanted to try one of those, and I've never been given a camera on an angel trip before. Suddenly I had an idea.

"Okay, Molly, sit over there," I said. "I'm taking your picture." Molly posed, and I clicked a picture of her in front of the fire. In a minute, her photo came out.

Her hair looked flame orange in the firelight, even though it was more blond in real life.

"Now, *you* take *my* picture," I said, handing her the camera. "If I'm an angel, my picture won't show up on film. I'll be invisible, like a spirit, right?"

Molly pretty much agreed. She snapped the picture, with me and the penny whistle. Sure enough, a minute later, there I was, Hannah Martin, in a photo.

"You're right," she said. "I suppose maybe you're not an angel after all." She sounded awfully disappointed. Well, it wasn't the first time I'd disappointed someone. I could handle it.

"Maybe we should work out a plan," I suggested. "You know, a real, human plan to find the thief and get the arts centre money back." (In case you're wondering, they spell the word "center" with an "re" at the end here in Ireland. I know you're reading this, Ms. Crybaby!)

"Good idea," said Molly. "Let's go talk to Uncle Seán. Kevin, can Hannah use your bike for a short while?"

"Sure," Kevin agreed. "Can Jimmy and I use this angel decoder thing while you're gone?"

"Why not?" I said.

"And your green pencils?" Jimmy added. "I want to draw the view out my bedroom window."

"Just be really, really careful with everything, okay?"

"Okay," they said in unison, excited.

Molly and I said good-bye to her mother, who was still dabbing at her eyes, and went out the front door. The family bikes were all leaning right there against the house. The Ryans didn't have a garage. There was a tiny, very cute-looking white car in the driveway. The steering wheel was on the right-hand passenger side. That's because, I already knew, they drive on the left side of the road in Ireland. Sounds pretty confusing to me. But hey, I wasn't going to be driving anywhere, anyway. I'm only in sixth grade, remember?

"The rain has let up, Hannah," said Molly. "I'll race you to Uncle Seán's house!"

"How far is that?" I asked.

"It's straight up that road, about four kilometers," Molly answered. I quickly did the math in my head. It kills me to admit it, but sometimes I'm actually grateful to Ms. Crybaby. If it weren't for her, I wouldn't know a thing about miles and kilometers. (Did you figure it out? Four kilometers equals two and a half miles.) I could handle two and a half miles. I thought.

"Okay, you're on!" I shouted, hopping on Kevin's blue bike. "But how do I know when I'm there?"

"Red door!" Molly yelled back. "And the last one there is a *firbolg!* Ready, steady, *go!*"

"A furball? Gross!" I said. These Irish people sure had some weird expressions.

"Not furball! *Firbolg,*" she shouted, passing

me. (I found out later what *firbolg* meant. You'll see when I show you my journal entry.)

Molly sped off ahead of me, and we were both out of breath when we pulled up to Uncle Seán's. We dashed in through the red door of his house.

"Uncle Seán!" Molly called.

At first I didn't even see him, his cottage was so packed with stuff. There were photos of Irish dancers on the walls, and pictures of musical instruments, and drawings of the new Celtic Arts Centre. Uncle Seán was sitting at his kitchen table sorting his CD collection, eating supper, and listening to flute music, all at the same time.

"Molly!" Uncle Seán said, jumping to his feet. "It's so good to see you! I've got a lot of nervous energy, and I don't know what to do with it. This missing money has got me all spun out."

"We're going to help you, Uncle Seán," said Molly. "This is Hannah Martin. The angels have sent her."

Uncle Seán's eyes twinkled. "Have they, now? Well, how do you do, heavenly Hannah Martin?" he said, shaking my hand warmly. With his other hand, he magically pulled a coin from behind my ear. "And you brought good luck with you, did you?" he said mischievously.

"I hope so," I said, laughing. I could tell already that Uncle Seán had the gift of gab, too. He was very young—probably Molly's dad's kid brother—with curly dark hair and sky blue eyes.

"So have your angels told you who the *real* thief is, now?" Uncle Seán asked. He was nervously twiddling the coin between his fingers.

"Or *thieves*," added Molly. "There could be more than one scoundrel involved."

"No, my angels haven't told me," I said. "They never give me any answers. But they'll help us figure it out."

Uncle Seán tossed the coin to me and nodded. "I have only till Sunday to find that money," he said. "Or there will be no arts centre." He started pacing the floor in front of his work table. "Come and look at this, ladies," he said.

On the table were a whole bunch of blueprints, the plans for the centre. From what I could tell, it was going to be very large, with ten sides. (David would know what you call that shape—I think it's a decagon.) There was a huge area for dancing, a concert auditorium, practice rooms, and even a little café.

"It looks awesome," I said.

"Seven years of hard work," said Seán quietly. "Here, let me show you how it looks on the computer. You can walk through it, room by room, and see the whole beauty of it."

He pulled up the image of the entrance, which had old Celtic designs around the door, and an art gallery as you walked in. As I was beginning to move through the gallery, something horrible popped onto the screen. It was an ugly leprechaun face, with a hideous grin. The leprechaun started laughing out loud—and talking!

The leprechaun

(Nasty grin, huh?)

"'Tis a pity you lost your pot o' gold, Seán Ryan," he taunted. Then the leprechaun threw back his head, snickering nastily. With a wink of his eye, he flashed off the screen. I stared at the monitor, still in shock.

"Well, of all the...!" blustered Uncle Seán. "It must have been the thieves themselves who put that on here!"

Uncle Seán quickly scooted me out of the chair and sat down. He started punching computer keys, trying to bring the nasty leprechaun back. "Nothing! It's gone! Why, those low-down, conniving robbers!"

"How did they get access to your program?" Molly asked, her voice trembling a bit.

"And who could they be?" asked Uncle Seán.

"And how can we find them?" I asked.

Just then, the screen started flashing. It turned golden white. We had to cover our eyes, it was beaming so brightly.

"Travel with Uncle Seán on his bread route tomorrow," said a voice. I recognized it right away.

"Demi!" I shouted gleefully. "Who put that leprechaun on the computer?"

But as fast as she had shown up, Demi disappeared. The screen went back to the entrance of the arts centre.

Uncle Seán frowned. "What was that?"

"It was one of my angels! Do you deliver bread?" I asked eagerly.

"Sure and I do, every morning, out along the coast and back," answered Uncle Seán.

"That bright light...that flash..." said Molly. "That...was one of your angels?" Her eyes were huge. She couldn't believe she'd just heard from a real angel.

"It sure was," I said. Then I turned all business. We had work to do. "Someone on your uncle's route may have information about the thieves."

"All of the towns in the area are involved with the new Celtic Arts Centre in one way or another," said Uncle Seán.

"So Molly and I will go with you tomorrow," I said. "We'll keep our eyes and ears open for clues while you make your deliveries."

"I don't know," Uncle Seán said slowly. He ran his fingers through his curly hair, seeming worried. "I don't want the two of you mixed up in this. It could be dangerous."

"We promise not to do anything rash," said Molly.

"Molly girl, I know ye," said Uncle Seán, tweaking her nose. "'Trouble' could be your middle name. You enjoy adventure. And just looking at Hannah, I can tell you're two of a kind, you are."

How could he tell that, just by looking at me?

"We'll be very, very careful," I promised in my most serious voice.

Uncle Seán shut down his computer and thought for a minute. "I could use all the help I can get, I suppose," he said. "Half-four it is, then." Half-four? He had to mean four-thirty. In the morning? Ugh. "I'll pick you two up in my lorry."

"Lori?" I asked. I was thinking about one of my other angels, Lorielle.

"My truck," said Uncle Seán. "We call it a lorry: L-O-R-R-Y."

"Oh," I said. I'd have to write that one down. I needed to start a list of Irish words and expressions while I was here. Just like on my mission in Australia, the version of English here sure was different from ours in America.

"Whew! I'm feeling tired just thinking about getting up so early," I added.

"Bone tired," added Molly. "But I'm hungry, too."

Uncle Seán dished us up bowls of delicious lamb stew and soda bread, which we downed in a matter of minutes with a cup of tea. Then we hurried back to Molly's house for the night. I wrapped up in blankets on the floor by the fireplace, in spite of the family's protests.

"The least I can do is give you a hot water bottle," said Mrs. Ryan. She tucked me in, with a warm rubbery sack by my feet. Even though we'd need to make an early start in the morning, I wasn't quite ready to go to sleep yet. The tea must have woken me up a bit. I pulled out my journal to start a new page. Jimmy and Kevin had left the angel decoder and pencils out for me, so I chose emerald, kelly, and spring green to write with.

> IRISH ENGLISH
> lorry = truck
> ceili = dance party (you say it KAY-lee)
> firbolg = early Irish settler who in legends is
> a short, lumpy creature with a potbelly
> (you say it fur-BULL-ig)

For some reason, I decided to try working on my peace poem again. But as I started to write, the weirdest thing happened. My hand began trembling, shaking like crazy. At first I thought I was cold, but no. Something else was going on. You'll probably think I'm nuts—but this is absolutely, positively true.

The words were writing themselves!

Chapter 5

Off in a Bread Truck

For a minute, I thought my angel Lorielle was helping me with my homework. Fat chance! Instead, here's what my hand wrote:

> In the west where fierce winds roar
> Lies the ancient rock of...

I could not read the next word. My handwriting was too scribbly, and the firelight was dim. It looked like "Inishmore." Couldn't be. That wasn't even a word.

"What ancient rock? Is it 'Irish lore'?" I asked Lorielle. But I didn't get an answer. Instead, my hand kept on writing more words.

> Seek the place of knowledge saved.
> One new stone has been engraved.

I scribbled and scribbled, really fast, by the firelight. Here's how Lori's message ended:

> No thief can steal the Celtic arts—
> Follow the rainbow, and your hearts.

This angel rhyme was like a riddle. What did it mean? I had a terrible urge to wake Molly up, right that very second. But I thought I'd better wait till morning. After all, that was only a few hours away.

Half-four came very fast. It was raining again, a misty drizzle. I was thinking how it was half-ten at night back home, time for me to be in a deep, dreamy sleep. My angels were probably getting a big kick out of this. I imagined Demi sprinkling me with cold drizzle, enjoying every minute of it.

A little sprinkle

Uncle Seán pulled up in his green (of course) bread lorry, and Molly and I jumped into the front seat. He had it heated up for us. We drove into the first little town, and a sturdy shopkeeper came out and waved to us. Uncle Seán jumped down, opened the back of the lorry, pulled out some warm loaves of bread, and ducked into the shop. I reached into my knapsack and opened my journal.

"Look at this," I told Molly. "I got a message from one of my angels last night."

"How magical!" said Molly brightly. The girl seemed as excited about my angels as I am.

"Her name is Lorielle," I explained, showing Molly the poem. "She loves words and codes. She's the one who gave me the decoder. I always imagine that she lives in a humongous library, with books in every language, even ancient languages. Anyway, this time she gave me a message in English."

"It's a poem!" said Molly, clapping her hands. "I love poetry!" She read through it out loud, pausing at the place where I'd left a blank after "rock of..."

"So these are clues to help us clear Uncle Seán's name?" she asked.

"Yes," I said. "But we have to figure them out for ourselves. My angels never make it easy. They say it's the job of us humans to do the work on earth."

"Sure, we can do this!" said Molly. "First of all..."

Just then, Uncle Seán hopped back in the lorry, soggy and chilled. In his hand, he had a steaming cup of tea that the shopkeeper had given him. Molly and I quickly stopped our angel work. We didn't want Uncle Seán to think we were putting ourselves in any danger.

"Next stop, the Bayside Bed and Breakfast," he announced. He loved his work, I could tell.

"Look over there!" Uncle Seán went on. He sure was jolly so early in the morning. He had more gift of gab than me, I guess. "That's a bog."

We looked. The sun was rising, peeking through the gray clouds. Some people, looking golden in the sunrise, were already working.

"They're cutting bricks of peat from the soft areas of the land," Uncle Seán explained.

"I know that," said Molly.

"Of course you do," said Uncle Seán. "But Hannah doesn't. So share your knowledge with her. It's our tradi-

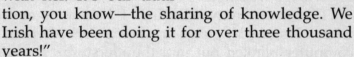

Cutting peat

peat ↓

tion, you know—the sharing of knowledge. We Irish have been doing it for over three thousand years!"

"Sorry, I wasn't thinking," said Molly. She looked at me. "We use the peat for fuel."

"You don't burn wood?" I asked.

Uncle Seán shrugged. "Why cut down trees if you can use peat from the earth?" he asked. Well, that made sense. I'll have to ask my dad if we can cut chunks of our garden soil and burn them in our fireplace at home.

Uncle Seán stopped the lorry and jumped out again. This was a big delivery—about two dozen loaves of bread. That gave Molly and me more time to work on the rhyme.

"It's true, what my uncle says about knowledge, Hannah," she said. "It's there in your message from Lorielle: 'the place of knowledge saved.' It's got to be a monastery. Did you know that centuries ago, monks copied books written by the Romans and Greeks?"

"No," I said. "But what does that have to do with Uncle Seán?"

"Well, I'm not certain," said Molly. "The point is, many books were destroyed when ancient Rome burned, and then there were wars. But luckily the Irish monks had already copied a lot of the writings. It was like having them saved on a back-up computer disk."

"So if it hadn't been for the monks, all that knowledge would have been lost?" I asked.

That was pretty amazing. I had a fit once when I lost my language-arts homework after our computer blinked out in a thunderstorm. It was just gone. Lost in cyberspace. And Ms. Crysler is not a person to take excuses. I got my one and only "F" ever on that project. Too bad I didn't have a monk in my basement, copying my homework.

"So I'm sure this angel message means we have to go to a monastery," said Molly.

"It does?" I asked.

A monk in my basement

"'Seek the place of knowledge saved...'" she repeated. "A monastery is the place where the monks copied all those books."

"So where is this monastery?" I asked.

"It could be anywhere," said Molly. "There are hundreds of them."

"Oh great!" I moaned.

Uncle Seán was back. This time he brought us some breakfast: cups of oatmeal, with thick Irish bacon on the side. His customers fed him like a king.

At the next stop, Molly and I read through the first stanza:

> In the west where fierce winds roar
> Lies the ancient rock of...

"Of *what?*" asked Molly. "I can't read this. You have frightful handwriting, Hannah."

"I can't read it either," I admitted. "It rhymes with roar. It might be 'Irish lore.'"

"Well, let me think," said Molly. "Irish lore...There's the Blarney Stone..."

"My friend David back home always tells me I must have kissed the Blarney Stone before I was even born," I said. "He says I'm full of blarney, that I have the gift of gab."

Molly laughed. "Sure now, I'd have to agree with him, Hannah. The only thing is, the Blarney Stone isn't in the west where the fierce winds roar. The weather is calmer down that way. It could be a rock on the far west coast someplace. It's a bit stormy and gray over there."

"But what other rock besides the Blarney Stone is in Irish lore?"

Just then, Uncle Seán waved us inside to the shop. He looked upset. We hopped out of the lorry and into the warm shop. It was a little café, with tables and lots of books to read while you had your tea.

"This is Kate O'Malley," said Uncle Seán, introducing us to the shopkeeper. "She's had some disturbing news this morning."

The gray-haired woman was wringing her hands. "They say the money for the Celtic Arts Centre is missing," she said. "And we got a call from the *gardaí* in Galway. Someone has reported that Seán here is the thief."

"What's the 'guard-ee'?" I asked. (I didn't know you spelled it *"gardaí"* until Molly told me later, when I added it to my Irish/English list.)

"The police," said Uncle Seán.

"They want to take Seán in for questioning," said Mrs. O'Malley. "This is outrageous! Somebody's out to frame you, Seán Ryan, that's what I think!"

"I can't believe this," Uncle Seán said, sounding very sad. "Who would try to frame me? And why?"

"Some hooligan who thinks he can run off with the loot while you sit locked up and lonesome," Mrs. O'Malley said, folding her arms.

It was terrible to think of nice Uncle Seán being locked up and lonesome.

"I don't think it's safe for you to be finishing your rounds, now," said Mrs. O'Malley. "Let my son Conor do it, will you?"

Lonesome Seán

"I couldn't do that," said Uncle Seán sheepishly. "I'd be putting him out…"

"Nonsense!" said Mrs. O'Malley. "What are friends for, anyway? We want to help you, Seán Ryan."

"All right," Uncle Seán agreed. "Just for today."

"You might want to make yourself scarce for a few days so the *gardaí* don't find you. They can spend their time chasing the real thieves, then," said Mrs. O'Malley.

"Perhaps the right thing would be for me to turn myself in," said Uncle Seán. "After all, I'm innocent."

Molly and I looked from Uncle Seán to Mrs. O'Malley and back again. This was awful.

"What good would it be to have you sitting in jail, Seán? No. Your friends will do whatever we can to help the *gardaí* find the real scoundrels and clear your good name."

Uncle Seán nodded slowly. "I suppose there's no harm in it, then."

"Now, I'll get my son Conor," said Mrs. O'Malley. "You three wait right here."

As we stood there, I flipped through the brochures on the tourist rack. Something was strange about the letters on one of them. They looked like angel code! I blinked and looked again.

"Molly!" I whispered. "Come here!" I picked up the flyer and showed her.

Her eyes just about popped out of her head. "It's your angel code, Hannah!"

It read:

o|o ♡ o|o ♭ ♪ a̲ -◦- ☺ ☆

Inishmore

Chapter 6

o|o ♡ o|o ♪ ♪ᵃᵃ ⋮ 🐾 ☆

"Give me that a moment," said Molly. "Let me try." She turned the decoder and got the very same word that I had: INISH-MORE.

"That's it!" she said excitedly. "That's the word!"

"What does it mean?" I asked.

My angel decoder

"Inishmore is one of the Aran Islands. It's a rocky island off the western coast, with high cliffs dropping down to the sea."

"So it has to be the place Lorielle was talking about in the poem!" I said.

"Exactly," said Molly, nodding. She recited the lines out loud:

"'In the west where fierce winds roar
Lies the ancient rock of Inishmore.'"

"So we need to go to Inishmore with your uncle, don't we?" I asked.

"I think so," said Molly. "Besides, it would be the perfect place for him to hide. It's very remote."

Conor came to the door just then, running his hands through his dark hair.

"Morning, Seán," he said, yawning. "I'll be finishing your bread route for you."

"That's good of you, Conor," said Uncle Seán. He turned to Molly and me. "I've got a plan, ladies," he said.

I almost said, *So do we!* But I held my tongue and let him talk first.

"Conor can drive us down to the ferry dock. I have an old friend, Brendan Flaherty, who runs the Inishmore Inn. I believe he would put us up for a night on the island while we put these puzzle pieces together."

Molly and I looked at each other, amazed. Had my angels planted this Inishmore idea in Uncle Seán's head, too?

"I'll lock your bread lorry in my garage," said Conor. "And I'll give it a good tune-up while I'm at it."

"Your garage is right by the ferry dock, isn't it?" asked Molly. I could tell she kind of liked Conor, even though he was probably eighteen. He did have a nice smile, I thought.

"Right," said Conor.

"Perfect," said Molly, giving him a big smile.

"Let's ring your mother before we go," said Uncle Seán, heading toward the phone, "to make sure this is all right with her."

Molly looked totally insulted. She probably didn't want Conor to think she was a baby, having to get permission from her mother.

"And what about you, Hannah?" asked Uncle Seán. "Should we ring your mother as well?"

"Uh...no," I stammered. "My mother's, uh, out of town. She knows where I am. It's fine."

"All right, then," said Uncle Seán. It was pretty much true. My mother *did* know where I was—at David and Katie's house. Angel time is very strange. Not a minute passes when I go on these trips. I always come back at exactly the moment that I left, in the very same place. Pretty much, anyway.

Conor drove, and I could tell he was nervous. He kept glancing in the rearview mirror, watching for *gardaí*. We got to the dock, and Molly's uncle jumped out.

"You two wait here a minute," he instructed.

We watched out the back window while Uncle Seán had a long conversation with the man at the ferry company. They looked like they knew each other. The man wrapped his arm around Uncle Seán's shoulder, shaking his head. That probably meant he sympathized with Uncle Seán. *It sure pays to have good friends when you're in trouble*, I thought. *Especially when it isn't your fault.* For some reason, I believed Molly's uncle. I was sure the angels wouldn't have sent me to help him and Molly unless he was innocent.

Uncle Seán waved for us to join him. When I got out of the truck, I was nearly blown over by the wind off the cliffs. I've never felt a strong wind like that. It's kind of scary.

"We're in luck!" Uncle Seán called. "The ferry is just about to leave."

"Good luck to you," said Conor. "I'll take good care of your lorry and your customers."

"Thanks," Uncle Seán told him. "Let's hope the angels are watching over us. We'll be back home tomorrow, in time for the big *ceili*."

"Cheers," Conor said, with a little salute. "And good luck."

Chapter 7

A Fairy Boat

The first time I ever heard of a ferry boat, I was five. I was crossing a river in Wisconsin with my mom and dad. I thought the word was "fairy," not "ferry." I watched the water for fairies, and I watched the sky, and I checked under people's feet. I was so disappointed when I didn't see even *one* fairy on that boat. When I told

Fairy Boat

David the story, he thought it was the dumbest thing he'd ever heard. Oh well. I can't think about David and his perfectly matched chess set just now.

Anyway, this time, on our way to Inishmore, I didn't bother to look for fairies. But I *did* bother to put on my yellow boots. They had thick fuzzy lining in them and felt pretty toasty in this freezing cold. The water sprayed up along the sides of the boat, so we stayed on the benches toward the inside, huddled against each other. The three Aran Islands grew larger as we approached. They looked like huge, jagged whales rising magically out of the wild sea.

"This is Inishmore?" I asked when we arrived. It was a little disappointing, I have to say. The island was all rocky, and gray, gray, gray. I didn't see one tree. It looked like we'd landed on the moon. "It's so bleak."

"Perhaps, but it's full of history," said Uncle Seán. I hoped I hadn't insulted him and Molly. "Aran is one of the oldest places of civilization," he went on. But I couldn't help thinking if I were an early explorer, I would not have chosen this gray, stony place to settle in. I would have built a boat and headed straight for the soft green of mainland Ireland.

After we got off the ferry, we piled onto a cart drawn by a small, very old-looking horse. We rolled through the town and stopped in front of a hotel called the Inishmore Inn. It was bright white, with a thatched roof and a door the color of my shamrock pencil. I couldn't wait to get inside, where I knew it would be warm and cozy.

"Well, if it isn't Seán Ryan," Brendan shouted when he answered the door. He gave Uncle Seán a big bear hug. "Come in out of that cold, now, all of you." That sounded good to me.

We went through a short hall into a big dining room with a fireplace. The walls were lined with bookcases. There were books floor to ceiling, end to end. I felt right at home.

"So, what brings the likes of you to my humble home?" Brendan asked. While Uncle Seán filled Brendan in on the whole story, Molly and I had cocoa by the fire—they call cocoa "drinking chocolate" here. For some reason, the chocolate tasted better in Ireland.

"How about a game of chess?" I asked her, eyeing a board in the corner.

"Why not?" she said. We set up the pieces, which were made out of green marble. The queen was beautiful. She looked a lot like David's missing queen, except she was loden-and-pine-colored, instead of black. (I'm really getting good with my greens on this trip, huh?)

"It's made of Irish marble," Molly said. "From Connemara, where we were today." Every piece in the set matched, of course. David would have been very happy. We had a great game, with no fighting at all, just fun. I hadn't played chess in ages, since David is the only person I know who plays.

"This is an outrage!" we heard Brendan boom as he tossed more peat on the fire. He was really angry, hearing Uncle Seán's story. While the two of them talked about how to save the arts centre, Molly and I began our chess game. But I was having a hard time concentrating. Molly captured a

whole bunch of my pieces right off the bat. I
didn't want to quit and seem like a poor sport or
anything, but I couldn't help eyeing all of
Brendan's bookcases.

Molly must have noticed. "We can finish our
game later," she said, after she swooped down
and took another one of my pawns with her
bishop. "Why don't we give those bookshelves a
look?"

She must have read my mind.

There were so many books, I wanted to stay
there for days and days, reading. A lot of them
had leather covers, and some of them had pages
with gold edges. First, I pulled out a book about
Aran sweaters.

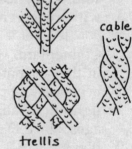

Some Aran stitches

tree
of
life

cable

trellis

"Hey, this is just like the
sweater you loaned to me,
Molly!" I said.

Molly nodded. "They knit
them here on the islands," she
said. "Years ago, each family knit-
ted their own designs. That way,
if a fisherman was drowned at
sea, they could identify him by the
knit of his sweater. Then they
could send his body back to his family."

"How terrible!" I said, horrified. "Did a lot of
fishermen drown?"

"All the time," said Molly. "The Atlantic is a
treacherous ocean, you know."

I shuddered and checked the designs on my sweater against the designs in the book. Sure enough, every single stitch had a name.

When I'd had enough of the sweater book, I explored the shelves some more. Then I found something incredible! It was a big, cloth-covered book in some ancient-looking language, with curly, graceful lettering. It looked as if it could have been written by angels. It wasn't in angel code, though.

"Oh, the Book of Kells!" said Molly, excited. "The original is kept safe in Dublin, our capital city. This is a copy."

"It sure is old," I said. "Look at these beautiful pictures!" Every page had magical pictures, with borders that braided in and out. Even the letters were made into pictures. I just *had* to pull out my journal and try to write my name Celtic-style. After I wrote it, I filled the spirals in with every shade of green from my pencils.

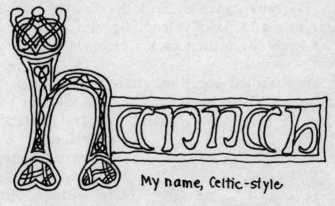

My name, Celtic-style.

Molly peered over my shoulder. "Remember when I told you about the monks writing down the knowledge of Europe?" Molly asked. "This is how they did it, with pictures and all."

Paging through the Book of Kells and writing my name ancient-style made me know this writing and drawing were somehow connected to Lorielle's message. It was just a feeling I got. I had to go exploring. I had to go *now*.

An angel from the Book of Kells

"But where will we go?" asked Molly. "We still haven't made sense of that poem."

"Let's take it one step at a time," I said.

Molly frowned, thinking. "All right, then, the first stanza led us to Inishmore."

"And here we are!" I said.

"The next stanza is: 'Seek the place of knowledge saved...'" Molly leapt up and grabbed a map from the tourist rack. "Here, let's look at this!" she said.

We huddled together, studying the map of Inishmore. There were ancient ruins all over the island: forts and churches and monasteries.

"We're heading for a monastery, a place where the

Δ = Ancient ruins

monks copied down all that knowledge," Molly said.

"Could that be it?" I asked, pointing to a larger ruin. The name was written in Gaelic, so I couldn't read it.

"That looks like an ancient church," said Molly. "It could be it. But so could this. Or this..." She pointed out several other ruins. Any of them could be a place where manuscripts were copied.

I sighed. "Well, all we can do is try them, one at a time," I said. At least the island of Inishmore was pretty small. We could probably check out the whole place, if we had to.

"We have no time to waste," said Molly, all business now. She gathered her sweater, boots, and jacket. They were nice and dry from the fire.

"If you're going out," Brendan called after us, "get yourself some grub from the pantry to sustain you."

Molly went to pack bread, chocolate, and cheese, and I bundled up. I stashed the map in one of my boots—they call them "Wellies" here, short for "Wellingtons," Molly says.

Brendan came over to whisper a word of warning. "Be careful out there," he told me. "The sea and the cliffs can be treacherous, Hannah. Don't forget that, not even for a moment."

Chapter 8

Hannah Martin,
Tribal Warrior

Brendan gave us two old bikes, and we raced down the roads between the stone fences. Every time we passed someone, they called, "Jay A Ditch!"

Ditch? I thought, feeling a little worried.

"Actually, it's spelled '*Dia huit*,'" said Molly. "It means 'hello' in Irish, or Gaelic." This was very confusing. Ancient languages aren't pronounced anything like you'd guess from the spelling!

I got into it, and started answering like Molly did.

"Jay A Ditch," someone would say.

"Jay A Is Mare A Ditch," I answered everyone. They smiled, so I guess I got it right. It means something like "Hello to you, too."

We came to a fork in the road.

"Which way?" I asked.

"It doesn't matter, really," said Molly, pulling out the map, which was sticking out of my boot. She pointed to the different ancient ruins we had talked about.

"Okay, let's flip a coin," I said. "Heads we go right, tails we go left." I dug into my pocket for the coin Uncle Seán had pulled from my ear. It came up tails. (Or, I should say, it came up harp. That's what's on the back of Irish coins. Underneath the harp, it said *Eire*. That's "Ireland" in Gaelic.)

We rode on that path to the left for way too long. I was very sorry we went this way. I was weary already. Molly, however, was doing just fine. Her cheeks were all rosy from the damp weather. It looked as if she could go on biking for miles more.

Soon we realized we were at the high cliffs of the west coast, over-looking the ocean. The sea was as gray as the sky and the stones. Wild waves splashed up against the rocks, far below. Right on the edge we could see a walled-in ruin, with smaller walls inside it.

Me & Molly out on the cliffs

Atlantic Ocean

"Is this the monastery we're looking for?" I asked.

"I don't think so," said Molly, checking the map. "I think this might be the Black Fort. The guidebook says part of the fort fell into the sea more than a hundred years ago."

Brrr! That gave me chills. I hoped we weren't going to fall into the sea. We had just finished inching our way to the cliff's edge. It was a l-o-n-g drop, straight down, to the Atlantic. I felt like I was standing at the edge of the earth. I imagined what it would have been like seeing the whole side of a huge stone fortress tumbling into the sea. Molly and I had to yell to hear each other over the crashing waves below.

"If we fall in and get lost at sea, at least they'll be able to identify us by our sweaters," Molly joked. I think she was joking, anyway.

"Not funny," I said, staring straight down at the deadly waters. I'm not usually afraid of heights, but I was getting all creeped out right now, just thinking about it. And to make matters worse, a thick fog was rolling in.

Molly noticed that, too. "Let's get out of here and head south before this fog overtakes us," she said. "There should be a monastery not far from here." But it was too late. Almost before she had finished speaking, the fog completely covered us in one sweeping minute like a thick wool blanket. We couldn't tell north from south, or east from west. Or see where the ocean was. I could hear it, though, pounding away against the rocks. We stood dead still.

"I'm scared," I whispered.

"Me too," said Molly.

"We'd better stand right here until the fog clears," I said. "Otherwise, one wrong step, and we could plunge straight down off the edge."

We didn't move. We didn't talk. We waited for the fog to move on. But instead of its clearing, the most amazing thing happened.

Right before our eyes, a group of gigantic stones rose slowly in front of us, straight out of the silent fog. There were about a dozen of them, standing up on end. They were much taller than Molly and I, and they seemed to be arranged in a sort of a ring.

"What in the world...?" I said, totally in awe.

"How strange!" said Molly. "These are stand-ing stones!"

"Standing stones?" I repeated. "What are those?"

"Nobody really knows," said Molly. "Ancient people put stones this way. You can see them in dif-ferent parts of Ireland. But there's something, I'm

Standing stones

afraid, that's not quite right...."

I didn't want to hear what was not quite right. This was all strange enough.

"How very odd. These standing stones weren't marked on the map," said Molly.

"And they rose right up in front of our faces, out of nowhere," I added. How could they do that? Had the angels done this? Was it a sign? Or was Demi playing some kind of joke on me?

"Let's step inside the ring," said Molly. She took a cautious step toward the huge stones. I didn't want to move. At all. But I wasn't going to stand still and watch my friend disappear into the fog, leaving me behind. I took a step forward, too. Now we were right in the middle, surrounded by a circle of ancient monster rocks.

"They look like soldiers, standing around us to protect us," I said.

Molly giggled nervously. "I was thinking the same thing myself," she agreed.

I stretched my arms out to the sky. "I'm an ancient warrior!" I said. "A warrior woman."

"That's funny, Hannah," Molly said. "Because your last name—Martin—is the name of one of the twelve ancient tribes of Galway. Did you know that?"

"I'm part of a *tribe?*" I asked, amazed.

"That's right," Molly said. "At least your ancestors were."

Wow! That was really cool! I began to imagine

what Hannah Martin, tribal warrior, would have worn and whom I would have been at war with. Maybe I would have been a really wild barbarian. Ms. Crybaby sure thinks I am sometimes.

I let out a loud whoop, and it echoed against the foggy circle of stones.

Just then Molly's eyes popped wide open. "Look, Hannah!" she cried. "The stones have some kind of writing on them!"

Me, tribal warrior

Chapter 9

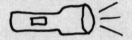

An Ancient Message

I dropped my warrior act and joined Molly by one of the huge rocks. I sure didn't see any writing. Here's exactly what I saw:

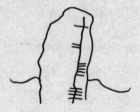

"It's Ome!" Molly said. "I learned about it in third class!"

"Ome? Third class?" I felt like Molly was speaking an alien language.

"Third class is your third grade," she explained. "We studied Celtic writing. The word is pronounced 'Ome' but is spelled O-G-H-A-M.

It's the lettering that the ancient Celts marked on the edges of stone pillars."

"Okay, so what does the Ogham thing *say?*" I asked, excited.

"I have to remember," said Molly, thinking. "It's been a long time, and I've never actually seen Ogham on stones before." She closed her eyes, trying to recall the ancient alphabet.

"Yes, I can picture my textbook," she said then. "A bit, anyway. I remember pretty well now." She stepped closer and studied the markings.

"It says 'Enda,'" said Molly.

"End of?" I repeated. "Like the end of the world?" That's where I felt we were right now—standing at the very end of the world, on the edge of a treacherous ocean. I was beginning to shake all over the place, and it wasn't from the weather.

"No," Molly corrected me. "*Enda.* That's the name of the saint who founded the Irish monasteries nearly fifteen hundred years ago!"

"So I guess we're right where we're supposed to be?" I asked, relieved.

Molly looked around, then checked the map. "I don't think so, Hannah," she said slowly. "Do you think this is another message from one of your angels?"

I knew she was right. Lorielle must have sent us the standing stones and the clue in Celtic writing. I reached into my backpack and fumbled for my camera. I wanted to shoot a picture to see if you could see the stones on film. I clicked a shot. Sure enough, nothing but a white fog showed up on the film.

"Thanks, Lorielle!" I said to the sky, shivering. At least maybe now we'd get on the right road. Molly pointed to a triangle on the map that showed the Church of St. Enda. It was way in the other direction, on the left fork of that road we had taken miles back.

"I'm sure we have to go back east, by the bay," said Molly.

I think maybe I moaned a little. But moaning wasn't going to save poor Uncle Seán. Then, as quickly as it had appeared, the fog disappeared, as if it was sucked up into the sky. The ring of stones faded instantly into nowhere.

We backed away from the crashing sea, hopped on our bikes, and zoomed off to the east. Pretty soon, we came to another stone ruin. The whole roof of the old church was gone, but the walls were still standing. I guess the sea and the wild winds here in Ireland are pretty hard on old structures. They just wear down and crumble apart eventually.

"This is it!" cried Molly. "The Church of St. Enda! This has to be the place the angels were talking about."

All around us, it was bleak and foggy (again!). The only thing I could see was a bunch of rocks left in ruins. Lorielle had led us *here?* What in the world were we looking for?

"We have to look for the next clue," said Molly. She was really getting into this whole thing now. "The second line of that stanza is: 'One new stone has been engraved.'"

"Hmmmm…'new stone'…Do you suppose it's a gravestone?" I asked.

"Perhaps," Molly said. "There's supposed to be a graveyard here someplace."

I looked around. I couldn't see anything but white fog. It was almost as if it was following us.

"Do you have a torch in your backpack?" asked Molly.

Was she crazy? "I don't think so," I said. "Unless the angels threw one in while I wasn't looking." A torch is probably what I would have used if I was a tribal warrior thousands of years ago. I opened my pack and fished around in it again.

"There! They *did* give you a torch!" said Molly, pulling out my flashlight.

"Oh. You mean 'torch' is the Irish way of saying flashlight?" I asked.

Me with my torch

"Yes," she said. Another word for my list.

We turned on my torch and took a few steps outside the ancient walls. Soon we were in the middle of a cemetery, all right. It was filled with very old-looking headstones.

I was looking for one with an angel code on it. Molly was looking for one with Celtic markings. We weren't getting very far. The fog just kept getting thicker and thicker, and we were chilled to our bones.

"Maybe we should find shelter," Molly said.

"Okay," I agreed. We turned our backs to the wind and walked backward, trying to avoid bumping into the headstones. If we could get inside the old church walls again, at least they would break the wind a bit.

Just then, for a split second, the wind cleared the fog away where my torch was pointed. It shone on a grave with a new headstone on it.

I directed the torch slowly up and down the headstone. "Molly!" I whispered, reaching for her arm. My voice barely came out. My knees felt weak. What we saw made us both scream.

Chapter 10

Baby Pig Eyes

A crow screeched. The fog swirled across the gravestone, making the name stand out even more: NORA LYNCH.

"Come on!" screamed Molly. "Let's get out of here!"

You know when ants scatter, how they run around willy-nilly? Well, that's exactly what the two of us did. We wanted to get back to the church, but the fog was so thick we could barely see two steps in front of us. I was racing one way; Molly was racing the other. We clunked into gravestones and tripped over rocks, until finally...*Crash!* We collided smack into each other.

We both went down, groaning and holding our heads. The ground was all soggy. We lay there for a minute, flat on our backs, a fine rain drizzling onto our faces. Then we struggled to our feet, each holding onto the other's sleeve, and raced like maniacs to anywhere—as long as it was far away from Nora Lynch's grave!

Finally we reached the doorway of the monastery. We staggered through, beyond the damp cold of the stone walls. The whole place was spidery and dirty and creepy and old. And there was no roof, of course! But at least we were out of the graveyard. And we were together. We found our bikes and huddled there, against a wall, nibbling on our bread and cheese.

"Did we really see...what we think we saw?" I asked. My jaw was practically frozen from fright.

"I...I don't know," stammered Molly. "I hope not. Nora Lynch's grave? Maybe the fog fooled us, don't you think?"

"Maybe," I said slowly. I had to think this through. "Or maybe that was the grave of...a different Nora Lynch," I suggested.

"But did you see the date on that gravestone?" Molly asked.

"No," I admitted.

"Both Nora Lynches died the same day!"

Well, that was that. How could two people named Nora Lynch, both from Aran, die on the same day?

I still didn't want to believe what we'd just seen. "What if Nora Lynch was buried twice?" I asked.

"Once here, and once near my

house?" Molly looked skeptical.

"Okay. What if just *parts* of Nora Lynch's body were buried here, and..." Ooooh, I couldn't even think about that. I shut up. This was not a good time to let my imagination and my gift of gab go wild.

I glanced over at Molly. She was still huddled against the rocky ruins, looking miserable. Tears had begun to stream down her cheeks, and her face was bright red.

"I'm sorry, Molly," I said. "I didn't mean to upset you. That stuff I was saying about parts of Nora Lynch's body was dumb."

"That's not what's upsetting me," said Molly. It's poor Uncle Seán. We seem to be so far off track."

"I know," I agreed.

"And what if...we never find the thieves?" Molly whimpered. "What if there is no Celtic Arts Centre?"

"I know," I agreed.

Then she *really* started crying. "Worse yet... What if...Uncle Seán ends up going to jail?"

I pulled a paper napkin out of our lunch bag and handed it to her. Molly blew her nose, hard. I didn't know what I could say to make her feel better.

"We're far, far away from a solution," Molly went on, sniffling. "And for Uncle Seán, every single minute counts."

I remembered feeling just as Molly did once, when I was on my angel trip to Kenya. I was sure I could never, ever get the medicine that little African girl needed to save her life. That's when my friend Sala's dad told me something important. Now I sat down beside Molly and told her what he'd said:

"'Defeat and death are the same thing,'" I quoted. "That's what they say in Kenya."

That made Molly cry even more. She sniffled into the napkin and rubbed her eyes, which were all red now. I felt terrible.

"We have a saying here in Ireland, too," she said then. "Would you like to put it in your journal?"

"Sure," I said, fumbling in my backpack. My fingers were trembling from the cold, but I managed to open my notebook to a clean page. I handed Molly my evergreen pencil.

In Gaelic, she wrote: *"Char dúnadh dorus a ríamh nar fosgladh dorus eile."*

I did not even attempt to pronounce that. "What does it mean?" I asked.

"It means: 'There was never a door shut but there was another opened,'" Molly said. She sat up a little straighter.

It took me a minute to figure that out. I guess it meant if you lose one opportunity, another opportunity is right there, waiting for you. So what door was open for us now? I sure didn't see one.

"Do I have baby pig eyes?" Molly asked suddenly.

"What?" I said, drawing back.

"Are my eyes all pink and swollen, like a baby pig's?"

I giggled. "Yep," I said truthfully. "You have a major case of baby pig eyes."

I told her I'd have to tell my dad, who's a vet, about this diagnosis. "I have bad news," I could imagine my dad telling a sick pet's owner. "I'm afraid your hamster has a serious case of...baby pig eyes."

Molly started to smile. That made *me* feel better. I kept it going.

"Hey, even with your baby pig eyes, I bet Conor O'Malley would think you're cute," I teased.

Molly playfully punched my shoulder. Now we were both laughing. It felt great. A cloud seemed to be lifting. We leaned against each other, shoulder to shoulder.

"So what door is open for us now?" asked Molly.

"I guess we'll have to ask the angels," I said.

"Okay," Molly agreed.

It was the first time I had ever decided to talk to my angels with somebody else there with me. I wondered if they would answer. I sure hoped so.

Chapter 11

Molly Meets an Angel

"Demi!" I called, shivering against the old rocks. "Can you give us a hint? What door is open for us now?"

"Demi is one of your angels, right?" Molly asked.

"That's right. She's the one who gave us the computer message," I said. "Her real name is Demetriel, but I call her Demi for short."

Just then, there was a tug on my hair. "Look, Molly!" I said, pointing to some strands of my hair. They were sticking straight up. "That's what Demi does when she wants to get my attention."

"She pulls your hair?" Molly asked, amazed. "How peculiar!"

"Yeah," I agreed. "I don't like it much myself."

"You're on the right track," said a voice that I knew was Demi's. I looked up. There was my guardian angel, sitting right on the old stone wall. Or at least I *imagined* I could see her. I glanced over at Molly, and I could tell she'd heard Demi, too. She sat perfectly straight, with her mouth hanging open in wonder. She was wide-eyed, her eyes darting here and there, trying to see Demi.

"Nora Lynch will open the door," Demi said.

Demi on the wall

"What does *that* mean?" I asked. "How can Nora Lynch open the door? She's dead!"

"Use what you have been given…" said Demi. This was getting annoying.

"Like Hannah's charcoal, or her green pencils?" Molly asked.

"Exactly," Demi answered. "And what else?"

"Her camera?" Molly piped in.

"Very good, Molly Ryan," said Demi. I was a little jealous. My guardian angel was talking with somebody else and telling her how smart she was.

"How about the penny whistle?" I asked.

"Not right now, Hannah," Demi said. I was crushed. Molly had all the right answers, and I had a wrong one.

"So how do we use the camera and the colored pencils?" I asked, a little huffy.

"That's what you'll have to figure out for yourselves," said Demi. "And then you'll have everything you need to save Uncle Seán and the Celtic Arts Centre."

"So should we take a picture of Nora Lynch's headstone?" Molly asked.

"Good thinking," Demi answered approvingly. Molly reached out toward the wall, sweeping the air with her hands, trying to feel where the angel was.

But I knew that Demi was already gone. She always leaves abruptly. I folded my arms, feeling pretty ticked off.

"Isn't she irritating?" I complained. "She could at least be a little clearer about what we're supposed to do. Or give us a better hint."

"An angel!" Molly said dreamily. She wasn't even listening to me, she was so enraptured. "I can't believe I just talked to an *angel!*"

"Big deal!" I said, snorting. "I do it all the time." Boy, was I being a jerk! I suddenly realized I'd better be careful. My angels might decide not to send me on any more missions. What if they fired me and hired Molly instead?

"Sorry, Demi!" I called, to smooth things over. No answer. At least I didn't get another tug on my hair. I think I was in the clear with Demi.

"Wasn't she wondrous?" Molly said, still caught up in meeting her first angel. "Will she come back?"

"No, Molly," I said, a little too briskly. "Demi

gave us all the information she's going to give us right now. So we'd better put our heads together and think."

"Well, it's getting late. We need to get back to the inn and talk this over," said Molly. Her baby pig eyes had cleared up. She was all twinkly since she'd talked with Demi.

"You're right," I agreed. "Your uncle will probably be worried about us."

We followed the walled paths along the bay. The fog had completely disappeared. It turned out we were really close to town. I couldn't believe it.

We parked our bikes and barged in through the shamrock green door.

"Uncle Seán!" Molly called. "Brendan!" We rushed through the hall into the library. We were out of breath when we reached them.

"You're just in time for the *seíson!*" Brendan announced. He said it like "session." He had his fiddle in his hand, and Uncle Seán was tooting on a penny whistle. A lady was playing the big harp in the corner, and a man was strumming a mandolin.

harp

fiddle

mandolin

"Session?" I said. "You mean, like practice?"

Uncle Seán stopped tooting and nodded.

"The Aran step dancers will be here any minute," he said.

"They've got to be ready for the Celtic Arts Centre *ceili* tomorrow," Brendan explained. "We're not going to let some thieving rogues stop our centre dead in its tracks!"

"But we've got to talk to you, Uncle Seán," said Molly.

"There's something important..." I started to say. But just then, the dancers started filing in through the front door. They were wearing dark green costumes with bright Celtic designs sewn along the edges. I sort of felt as if Molly and I were in the way. We stepped aside and let them march into the dining room–library.

"Welcome, all!" Brendan greeted them.

Uncle Seán's sky blue eyes were lit up like stars. This excitement was probably good for him. He needed to believe the Celtic Arts Centre was really going to be built. He needed to forget about the theft and the gossip—and jail—for a couple of hours.

"After the practice, we'll have time to talk," Uncle Seán told Molly and me.

The two of us looked at each other. What could we do? We didn't want to spoil the moment. But we were bursting to tell him about Nora Lynch's grave.

Now the music was starting. We would just have to wait.

Chapter 12

A Little Dance Practice

"Get into your costumes, girls!" Brendan called to us. He was taking charge of the evening, bossing around the musicians and the dancers, and setting out a bunch of food.

Costumes? What was he talking about?

Molly grabbed my arm and led me upstairs.

"My costume is at home, but we can use whatever we can find in the wardrobe here," she said. She pulled out a traditional Aran costume. It had a red flannel skirt, black tights, and a black and red shawl.

"Can you imagine climbing up and down those cliffs wearing all this?" she asked.

I shook my head. No way. I'd be tripping on the skirt, losing the shawl, and tumbling right off the rocks down to the ocean.

I picked out a green costume with shamrocks

on it, and a white cape with more shamrocks. We put on clunky black shoes with little taps on them and hurried downstairs.

The *seíson* was in full swing. There was enough tapping and stomping going on to wake the dead.

"I have no idea how to step dance," I told Molly. "You do know that, don't you?"

My shamrock costume

cape

Molly smiled. "Come over here in the corner, and I'll show you a few steps," she said. She held her arms straight to her sides and started moving her feet so fast it looked like she had six legs, I swear!

"I can't do that!" I complained. I wished that Katie were here. She's a great dancer, and she can pick up any step really easily. Dancing is not exactly my best talent.

Molly slowed her pace for me.

Molly's 6 feet

"Try this, Hannah," she said. "Hop, two-three."

I hopped two-three. So far, so good.

"Now hop, two-three and a-hop, two-three."

My feet a-hopped-two-three right over each other and tripped me, facedown, onto the floor.

"I'm such a klutz!" I moaned.

"No, you're not," said Molly, helping me back on my feet. "Irish dancing is hard at first. I've been doing it since I was a wee girl."

We practiced until I could hop-two-three-and-a-hop-two-three pretty well. It was called a jig, Molly said. Watching the other dancers helped me, too. Pretty soon, I was jigging around to the music, no matter what they were playing.

The step dancers did reels and hornpipes, too, which were much more complicated than my little jig. They danced in a line, and they danced in a circle, and they danced alone, and they danced together, eight at a time. They were great!

I sat on the floor, drawing them with my colored pencils. I had the perfect shade for every green.

"I don't want to put a damper on the festivities," Brendan finally announced, late in the evening. "But I want you all to know what's happened to our friend Seán Ryan."

Everybody stopped their strumming and tooting and dancing, and listened while Brendan told them the whole sad story. He walked over to his computer and pulled up the plans for the arts centre for everyone to see.

Everybody gasped. The nasty leprechaun was back, his face flashing on the screen! "'Tis a pity you lost your pot o' gold, Seán Ryan," the ugly little man taunted again. Then, with a snicker and a wink, he was gone.

"This is an outrage!" said Brendan.

Everybody agreed. "How can we help?" **someone asked.**

"We'll let you know tomorrow at the *ceili*," Brendan said. "Surely we'll do everything we can to find the money and bring these thieves to justice!"

After everyone had pledged their support, they went home, promising to be at the dance on Sunday.

"Time to turn in, now," Brendan told us.

"No!" Molly and I both said at once.

"We told you, we need to talk to you," Molly said. "It's really important!"

"It's true. The girls have been waiting all night to tell us something," said Uncle Seán.

"All right, then," said Brendan. He got us some drinking chocolate, and the four of us gathered in front of the fire. "Please begin, ladies."

It was weird being called a lady. But it was kind of nice, too. I felt very grown-up.

"I don't know how this will help you, Uncle Seán," Molly began, "but Hannah and I have been to a cemetery. We found a gravestone with the name Nora Lynch!"

By Brendan's fire.

Chapter 13

Back to the Boneyard

"So?" Uncle Seán asked.

I felt a little disappointed. I was hoping somehow that Nora's name would cause a big reaction.

"Who *is* Nora Lynch?" I asked.

Brendan leaned back in his chair.

"She was a very lovely woman who lived on the island all her life. A fine artist, she was," he said. He raised up his mug to toast her memory. We all clinked cocoa cups.

"Nora spent her last years painting the grand seascapes on Inishmore," Brendan continued. "I have three of her paintings here at the inn, in fact."

"Those big oil paintings I saw in the hall?" I asked.

"Indeed," said Brendan. He sighed. "Poor Nora. She passed on just last week."

Molly and I exchanged a look.

"And where was she buried?" Molly asked.

"Down by the sea, of course," said Brendan.

"But didn't she always want to be buried on the mainland, where it's green?" I asked.

"No, no!" said Brendan. "Nora loved the sea. In fact, she's buried in that old cemetery near St. Enda's."

Aha! I thought. So Molly and I *had* seen what we thought we'd seen!

"Ay, she'll be resting in peace there," Uncle Seán said.

"I don't know about that," I said slowly. Uncle Seán and Brendan both looked at me and frowned.

Molly leaped up and started pacing. "Could there be another Nora Lynch who was buried yesterday, by the hill in *our* cemetery back home?" she asked her uncle.

"That wouldn't make sense, now, would it?" Uncle Seán said, chewing on the tip of his pipe. "There was no Nora Lynch who lived in our town. No, I don't believe so."

Now I was on my feet, too, pacing beside Molly. "But there *was* a Nora Lynch buried there yesterday! Her family said she always wanted to be buried in a green place," I rushed on.

"So they took her from Aran and buried her in Galway," said Molly.

"That wouldn't make much sense either,"

mused Uncle Seán, "if this Nora Lynch loved Aran so much."

"But what if they *did* take her to Galway? Then who is buried in the grave here on Inishmore?" I asked.

Brendan held up one hand for us to slow down. "Nora Lynch is definitely buried here, right over by St. Enda's," he said.

"You're sure?" I asked.

"I swear on my own mother's grave," he said. "I was at Nora's funeral. I helped to carry her coffin."

"Then who was buried yesterday in Galway, in Nora Lynch's grave?" I asked.

We looked at one another, befuddled.

"Who buried Nora Lynch in Galway?" asked Brendan.

"And how do you girls know about it?" asked Uncle Seán.

We told them about seeing Nora's family members, dressed like blackbirds. "They were tall and thin, with black hair—" I went on.

"That's enough," said Uncle Seán, jumping up from the table. "Come on. We're going back to that boneyard! We must make sure poor Nora's grave hasn't been tampered with!"

We all jumped up to follow him.

"No, Seán," cautioned Brendan. "You stay right here, where it's safe. If the *gardaí* come looking for you, hide in the pantry."

Uncle Seán hung his head woefully. "This is a terrible thing," he mumbled. "You take care of those two girls, Brendan. Don't let them get into any trouble, now."

"I'll keep two good eyes on them," Brendan promised. "We'll be back in an hour. Come on, girls, we'll take my tour bus."

Molly and I raced out the door and hopped onto the bus behind Brendan.

"Let's take a picture of Nora Lynch's grave!" Molly whispered to me.

"What good will *that* do us?" I asked.

"I don't know," she said. "But Demi told us to use the camera, remember?"

"You're right," I said with a sigh. "If Demi thinks we should take a picture, we should do it." Even when my angels tell me to do the weirdest things, I do them. I have to trust what they tell me. Somehow, their instructions always seem to make things work out in the end.

We headed back in the direction of the cemetery. Now, in the clear moonlight, we could see the carving on all the old stones. Brendan hopped out of the bus and made a beeline for Nora Lynch's grave. Sure enough, there it was.

"Plain as the nose on your face," said Molly.

"It hasn't been touched, has it?" I said. The earth in front of the stone didn't look as if it had been tampered with.

"Nobody's tried to dig here," said Brendan.

"I have an idea," said Molly suddenly. "Give me that charcoal pencil of yours." I handed it to her. What was she up to?

"And I need four pieces of paper from your journal," she added. "And your tape."

"Yes ma'am," I said, giving a little salute. Molly paid no attention. I decided that I was just feeling jealous again. I was going to have to stop that. So what if Molly was doing a lot of work on this mission? I had to admit, she was doing a great job.

"Why don't you and Brendan stand over there, next to the gravestone?" I asked.

I dug into my backpack for the camera. *Click!* I shot a picture. While we waited for it to develop, Molly taped the four pieces of paper together to make a large rectangle. Then she laid the paper over the writing on the grave.

"A fine, good idea!" said Brendan. "A grave rubbing."

I watched, fascinated, as Molly rubbed the whole surface of the stone with black charcoal. The letters showed up outlined, and lighter than the rest of the stone. I remember doing something like that with leaves and crayons in second grade.

"Now we have an exact copy right on this piece of paper," said Molly, returning my charcoal.

Almost at the same instant, the photo came out. It was perfect!

Quickly and carefully, I stashed our evidence in my backpack to keep it dry. We had plenty of proof that Nora Lynch had been buried in Inishmore.

"Where are we going next?" I asked eagerly.

"Home to bed," Brendan said firmly. "Time to turn in after a long day."

"But we can't go to bed now!" Molly objected. "We haven't found the thieves, or the money!"

"And we have only until tomorrow to clear Uncle Seán's name," I added.

"So what are you two planning to do?" asked Brendan. "Stand around in the graveyard, waiting for the thieves to come and announce themselves to you?"

"No..." Molly and I both said at once. Brendan was right. We didn't have any idea where to go next. Not yet, anyway. How exactly were the photos and rubbings of Nora Lynch's grave going to save Uncle Seán?

We rode in miserable silence all the way back to the inn. Then Molly and I dragged ourselves up to our bedroom.

"I have an idea about a possible connection here," Brendan called up the stairs after us. "I'll sleep on it and let you know in the morning!"

I hoped he'd sleep on it well. Brendan's big idea seemed to be a faint ray of hope in this dreary mess.

Chapter 14

You Only Die Once

Early the next morning, there was a loud knock on our bedroom door.

"Get up, now, ladies!" Brendan called. "We're going visiting!"

Molly and I jumped out of bed, wriggled into our clothes, and followed Brendan out the front door and down the road.

"What is it, then, Brendan?" Molly asked as we practically ran along beside him. Brendan was a very fast walker.

"Nora Lynch's family all are light-haired, and always have been," he said.

I was too sleepy to figure out how that was important. But Brendan was already ahead of us again, hurrying down the road.

I was feeling a lot of pressure now, since I'd

been in Ireland for two whole days and hadn't come up with one real clue to help save Uncle Seán. But maybe Brendan's idea would help. And another good thing: The weather was beautiful! There were soft clouds in the sky that looked like angel wings. I watched them closely. Maybe Aurora would send me a cloud message, the way she did sometimes. But we arrived where we were going before I saw any sign from my angels.

Brendan stopped in front of a red door to a white house and knocked. A blond woman with green eyes (seafoam green, to be exact) answered the door.

"Well, if it isn't Brendan Flaherty himself," she said. "Come in for a cup of tea."

"Sorry, Mary, but I don't have time for a chat." He turned to Molly and me. "This is Mary Lynch. Nora Lynch's daughter." He filled Mary in quickly on the burial story. He told her about the blackbird Lynches, too.

"They said they were Nora's family," Molly added.

"Impossible," said Mary, frowning. "We Lynches all are light-haired."

"And they said they'd brought her from Aran to be buried," I added.

"Also impossible. Mum's buried right here on the island. Rest her dear soul." Mary's eyebrows creased together in an even bigger frown. "I don't want to make a wrong assumption," she said, "but I might know who was behind this burial. There was a raven-haired man I fired from the shop last week."

Molly and I nudged each other. It seemed we were onto something!

"He and a young lady and another lad tried to pinch some money from my shop, they did," Mary continued, "so I sent him walking."

"Do you remember his name, Mary?" asked Brendan.

"It was Seamus," she answered, pronouncing it "Shame-us." "And shame it is on all three of them!"

"Was he tall?" I asked.

"Tall, and very thin," said Mary. "And he knew my mum was being laid to rest."

"Do you know where they went from here?" Molly asked.

"They probably headed back to the mainland," said Mary, "looking for someone else to steal from, no doubt."

Right away, I thought of those thieves heading to the mainland to steal from Uncle Seán. The fund-raising for the Celtic Arts Centre was advertised on posters all over the county.

"So whom did they bury in Galway?" asked Mary Lynch. She leaned closer and lowered her voice. "You don't think they murdered someone, do you, now?"

A big chill ran through all of us at once. *Murder?*

"I don't think they murdered anyone," said Molly.

It was as if a lighthouse suddenly flashed its blinding beam right over my head. "I don't think they *buried* anyone, either."

Brendan understood me right away. His eyes gleamed. "Do you think they buried a coffin full of..."

Chapter 15

Dolphins Take the Lead

Molly and I sped off down the road before Brendan even finished his sentence. We had to get back to Galway immediately—if not sooner. We burst into the library, where Uncle Seán was reading.

"We're going back, Uncle Seán!" Molly shouted, running over to him.

"What happened?" he asked eagerly.

"We know who the thieves are!" I told him.

"Who?" demanded Uncle Seán. "What...?"

"Follow us!" Molly instructed. "We don't have time to talk."

Just then, Brendan hurried in the door.

"You can't take the regular ferry," he said. "The *gardaí* will surely be waiting at the other end to arrest Seán."

"Then what will we do?" asked Molly.

"I'll ring my friend," said Brendan, heading toward the old-fashioned-looking phone in the hallway. "He has a smaller boat that usually doesn't run this time of year. And I'll let Conor O'Malley know you're on your way!"

While Brendan made calls, we got our things together. We hurried down to a private dock, where the captain of the boat was waiting, surveying the sky.

"Storm's a-coming," he warned, shaking his head.

I didn't believe him. It was a little gray to the west, all right, but where we were looked fine. I thought he was being a bit pessimistic.

"We really should not go," the captain said.

"This is an emergency," Brendan insisted. "If you leave right now, you'll be fine."

"Life jackets for everyone, then," said the captain. "*On*," he added sternly to me and Molly. We boarded the little ferry and snapped ourselves into our bright orange life vests. "I don't know what this big emergency is, but it better be a matter of life and death!"

Well, it turned into a matter of life and death, all right. When we were halfway to the mainland, the weather turned for the worse. It was amazing

to watch. Within minutes— seconds, practically—huge dark clouds rolled in, a heavy rain started, and waves rolled up, like monsters from the deep. Unfortunately, on this little boat, there was no place to duck underneath for shelter.

"Hang on!" yelled the captain.

An hour before, the clouds had looked soft, like angel wings. Now they hung like a gloomy dark ceiling, dumping cold, hard rain on our heads. Even in my thick sweater and heavy boots, I was freezing. I swear my bones were shivering.

"We have to turn back!" the captain bellowed above the wind. "The storm's too fierce!"

The ferry lurched sideways, hurling Molly and me against the metal rail. We grabbed each other tight and planted our feet against the waves. The wind roared across the Atlantic, and the rain stung our faces.

Suddenly I heard an eerie sound through the rainy fog. It was a high-pitched cry, the exact sound of the E on my flute. (E, as you may already know, is my very favorite note!) I listened hard. *Eeeeee! Eeeeee!* I heard. What in the world...?

Maybe it was Lyra, sending me a musical message. Was she about to send me home because of the danger? *No!* I pleaded. *Don't send me home yet! I need more time. What about poor Molly and Uncle Seán?*

"Dolphins!" shouted Molly, pointing. She'd heard the sound, too! "It's the dolphins from Dingle!"

"Impossible!" the captain hollered. "They

never swim up this far north!"

But I had spotted the dolphins, too. Right where Molly was pointing, I could see fins diving and flashing through the wild waves.

"See?" shouted Molly. "I told you!"

"Saints preserve us!" yelled the captain. He spun the wheel of the ferry, trying to get out of the dolphins' path.

"They swam all the way from Dingle!" yelled Molly, jumping up and down. "Listen, Hannah! Can you hear? They came to bring us a message!"

It was hard to hear anything with the wind whipping past my ears. I watched as one dolphin swam right in front of the boat. The others gathered on either side of us.

"I can't turn the boat around!" yelled the captain. "The dolphins are in the way!"

Molly was ecstatic. "The dolphin in front is Fungi!" she shouted, racing as far as she could to the front of the ferry. "He's Dingle's special mascot."

Fungi was *eeee-eeee*ing all over the place. "He's telling us to keep going!" she yelled to the captain. "He'll lead us there safely!"

"How do you know what he's saying?" I asked her.

"Just look at him go! He keeps swimming toward the mainland."

I wasn't so sure about the idea of following a dolphin. I looked to the sky. Had my angels sent the dolphins? Suddenly, a rainbow arched over my head. It reached, violet-pink-orange-yellow-green-blue, across the bay to Galway.

Molly clapped her hands. "The angels," she said.

"Impossible," said Uncle Seán, sounding awed. "A rainbow in the middle of a heavy storm!"

But I knew it wasn't impossible. It was Aurora, letting us know for sure that Fungi really *was* going to lead us to the mainland safely.

The boat rocked and lurched all the way (and so did my stomach!), but finally we made it across. We all took a deep breath when we set foot on solid land, especially the captain. We thanked him, and he headed directly toward the nearest inn. Then Molly, Brendan, and I snuck around the back way to the garage where Conor had hidden Uncle Seán's lorry.

But the lorry wasn't there. Neither was Conor. Had something awful happened? I had a bad, bad feeling about this.

Chapter 16

The Rainbow

A car screeched up behind us.

"Get in!" hollered a woman. It was Kate O'Malley, Conor's mother.

We didn't ask any questions. Uncle Seán grabbed four shovels from Conor's garage and threw them in the trunk. We jumped into the little car, and Mrs. O'Malley took off up the coast, checking nervously in her rearview mirror all the way. She was driving as fast as she could without speeding.

"The *gardaí* picked up Conor for questioning," she told us.

"No!" cried Uncle Seán.

"And they confiscated your lorry," she added.

"I'm not going to let Conor pay for this mess!" Uncle Seán said firmly. "I'm innocent, and I'm turning myself in."

"You'll do no such thing!" said Mrs. O'Malley. "Brendan filled me in on what the girls have discovered. We're going to get to the bottom of this right now. We're following that rainbow all the way to—"

She slammed on the brakes. There, right in the middle of the road, was a flock of sheep. There must have been a hundred of them. They were baaing and wandering around like one huge pile of pillows.

"Come on, Hannah!" hollered Molly. "Get out!"

She jumped from the car, and I followed. We started pushing the animals gently to get them to cross the road. I was actually a little scared. Some of the sheep were huge, like wool monsters with four hundred legs! And their teeth were yellow, much bigger than I'd expected. I was afraid one might bite me, or get mad and start ramming me like a goat.

I marveled at the way Molly pushed the stubborn beasts around. She wasn't scared at all. We kept pushing and herding. Finally, the sheep crossed the road. We were on our way once more.

I looked up at the sky. Something was sparkling and dancing in the colors of the rainbow.

What an amazing sight! It was my—our—angels, guiding our way!

"Remember the last stanza of Lorielle's message?" I asked.

Molly recited it: "'No thief can steal the Celtic arts—Follow the rainbow, and your hearts.'"

We followed that rainbow, all right. It beamed a shining path straight to Nora Lynch's grave.

"Now what?" I asked as Mrs. O'Malley pulled the car into the cemetery.

"I think we'll get Mr. Sullivan, the grave-digger, to help us," said Uncle Seán.

"No!" Molly practically screamed.

"He was there, at the burial, Uncle Seán. He might be in cahoots with the thieves!" I said.

Uncle Seán's face dropped. "Michael Sullivan, a thief? Rubbish," he said.

"But why else would he have been watching me so closely?" I asked.

"And why else would he have been with those people at the burial?" asked Molly.

"Michael Sullivan?" Uncle Seán repeated, shaking his head. "I still don't believe it."

"I can't, either," said Mrs. O'Malley. "Why, he helped raise funds for the arts centre, didn't he?"

"Indeed he did," said Uncle Seán, nodding.

"Then he may have known exactly how much money there was," I pointed out. "Maybe he even knew you had the money at your house Thursday night, Uncle Seán."

Uncle Seán looked crushed. "My own friends, turning out to be thieves?"

I remembered my angel trip to Mexico, where someone I trusted got caught up with treasure thieves. "Sometimes even good people get tempted to do awful things," I said. Ever since that trip to Mexico, I'd been a lot more careful about whom I trusted.

We all looked around to make sure Mr. Sullivan was not anywhere in sight.

"I'd say the coast is clear," said Uncle Seán. He sounded very sad.

"I suppose we'll just have to dig up this grave ourselves, Uncle Seán," said Molly.

"All right. Let's get to work," said Mrs. O'Malley briskly. She unloaded the shovels from the trunk of her car.

We each grabbed a shovel and dug in. It was hard work. I was sweating all over the place under my sweater. I tried not to think about the fact that I was actually digging in a cemetery.

We were about halfway down when we heard footsteps.

I looked up from the grave. My heart almost stopped.

Standing right behind Uncle Seán, his arms folded across his chest, was Michael Sullivan. And he didn't look happy.

Chapter 17

Pot o' Gold

"Well, if it isn't your man Seán Ryan, digging up a grave," Mr. Sullivan said. "I wouldn't have believed it if I didn't see it with my own eyes."

Uncle Seán turned around very slowly. I saw his grip on the shovel tighten. Oh no! Maybe he was getting ready to konk Mr. Sullivan over the head.

"The thief himself," the gravedigger added. "Caught red-handed."

"Don't you have that wrong?" said Uncle Seán, stepping toward him. "It's you who's the thief, Michael Sullivan."

"What are you talking about?" demanded the gravedigger.

"You know perfectly well," answered Uncle Seán. "There's no Mrs. Nora Lynch buried in this grave."

Mr. Sullivan looked completely baffled. "Then who *is* buried in that grave?" he asked. "I dug it myself. I was there at the burial."

"Well, let's just find out for ourselves," said Uncle Seán.

We went back to shoveling.

"I've got a machine that will pull up that coffin a lot faster," said Mr. Sullivan. He seemed very uncertain.

"Go get it, then," said Mrs. O'Malley. "We don't have all day."

I must have held my breath the whole time the dirt got cleared. Soon a wooden coffin was lifted out and set down on the ground. I turned away. What if Nora Lynch *was* inside? Or parts of her…I really, really did not want to see this. Molly wasn't looking, either. She was gazing up at the sky. Was she calling the angels again?

our feet
by the
open grave

Slowly Mr. Sullivan pried off the lid of the coffin. I peeked. The inside of the box was filled with—rocks.

"The rocks made the coffin seem heavy, as if there was a person inside," Uncle Seán said. We started throwing the rocks out, one by one. I was so relieved that Nora Lynch wasn't there that I threw faster and faster. Then we found it: sure enough, a small yellow tin box.

"A biscuit tin!" whispered Mr. Sullivan. "It's the sly leprechaun's pot of gold, sure it is, then."

Uncle Seán lifted the lid off the tin. *Yes!* Inside was a whole bunch of money in bills and coins.

"The money for the arts centre!" said Uncle Seán joyfully. He began counting the stash. "It's all here!" he announced.

"I can't believe the rogues pulled such a trick on me!" said Mr. Sullivan, shaking his head.

"The hooligans were probably planning to come back and dig this up while everyone in the village was celebrating at the *ceili* tonight!" said Uncle Seán.

"Well, won't they be surprised?" said Mr. Sullivan, smiling slowly.

"Come on, let's go to the *gardaí*," said Mrs. O'Malley. "There's no more time to waste."

We piled into Mrs. O'Malley's car and headed to the *gardaí* station. Molly held the money tin in her lap.

The minute we got to the little station, we saw Uncle Seán's bread lorry parked outside. Two *gardaí* ran out and took hold of Uncle Seán.

"We've been waiting for you, Seán Ryan," said one.

"Sorry, Seán," the other said, "but we'll be needing to keep you here for a while."

"Just one moment, now," said Mr. Sullivan, emerging from the car. It had been a tight fit. "You won't be having to keep him at all. Have we got a tale to tell!"

The *gardaí* got Conor from the back room, and we sat down to tell them our story: Uncle Seán, Kate O'Malley, Conor, Mr. Sullivan, Molly, and me. We told them everything: about the blackbird people, and Nora Lynch, and the Inishmore grave, and the tin full of money.

"I've seen those people wandering around here since Friday. I wondered what they were up to," said one of the *gardaí*, nodding. "They looked suspicious to me, but I had no reason to question them."

"All right, then," said Mr. Sullivan. "We have a plan."

"The *ceili* will go on as scheduled," said Uncle Seán. "We just want to make certain our thieves come to the party."

"I'll see to that," said Mr. Sullivan. "They'll trust me. I'll pay them a visit and give them a special invitation. After all, everyone will wish to comfort the bereaved on their loss." He chuckled slyly.

"The grave will have to be filled in again quickly, so they don't suspect anything," I said.

"I'll see to that, too," said Mr. Sullivan.

"And we'll have a special dance, just for them," said Uncle Seán, winking at Molly.

"Come on, Hannah," Molly said excitedly, jumping up and grabbing my arm. "We need to get ready. We have a mission to accomplish."

I had no idea what was going on, but I was game. I followed Molly out the door.

Chapter 18

A Circle of Dancers

Everybody went to take care of their parts of the plan. I couldn't have told you what the whole plan was, because I didn't know myself at the time. All I knew was, I had to dance!

So here's how I got ready for my part in this whole thing:

I got dressed in my dancing costume again— the green one, with the shamrocks and the cape. It's actually called a stole, I think. It doesn't fly around when you're jumping up and down, because it's pinned at the shoulder and the waist. I practiced what Molly had taught me, with my arms straight at my sides and my feet doing all the moving. By now, I was getting pretty good at it, if I do say so myself.

Molly got into her costume, which

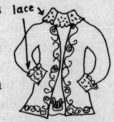

The Celtic costume

had more colors than mine, and Celtic designs like the ones in the Book of Kells. She looked really great.

We went over to the big hall where the *ceili* would take place. It was mobbed! People had shown up from all over County Galway! I guess everyone wanted to see the ancient Irish arts kept alive! The dancers all wore beautiful costumes, and the musicians were tuning up their harps and fiddles and mandolins. Someone had an accordion.

Brendan and the Aran step dancers were already there, and Conor and Kate O'Malley, and probably every person I had met the whole time I was in Ireland. I felt like I was in the middle of a family reunion.

I saw Uncle Seán talking with Michael Sullivan and some other men. All of them were dressed in tweed jackets and caps. I could swear I'd seen those men in the tweed before. I just couldn't place their faces.

In every corner of the room, something was going on. Everybody had a part to play, and they were being *very* secretive. Nobody was talking out loud about the theft. I felt like a spy.

Everything came together when the three thieves entered the room. They were still dressed like blackbirds, I guess because they were supposed to be in mourning. Michael Sullivan crossed the room, meeting them at the door as if they were the honored guests.

"Welcome, Lynch family!" he greeted warmly. "Please, come to a special table, right up front."

Michael, Uncle Seán, and the men in tweed sat with them. Just then, I suddenly realized who the tweed guys were!

"The *gardaí* from the station!" I whispered to Molly. I hadn't recognized them without their uniforms. Molly winked and put a finger to her lips. The blackbirds had no idea who the *gardaí* were, I could tell.

The music started up, and the show began. There were concertina players and fiddlers. There were pipes and whistles and bodhrans. (Bodhrans are like drums.) There were jigs and reels and hornpipes. There were dances in lines, and dances in circles.

Uncle Seán got up to talk about the Celtic Arts Centre as if nothing unusual had ever happened. There was no mention of the missing money.

"We'll have a very special dance now," Uncle Seán announced, "in honor of our visitors who recently lost their dear mother from Aran."

Everybody turned and looked at the three blackbirds.

"Molly?" Uncle Seán gave her the cue. "Dancers, please." We stood up—me and Molly and the Aran dancers. We got into a circle and waited for our cue.

Michael Sullivan very graciously took the arm of the lady blackbird. The *gardaí*, disguised in their tweed jackets, took the arms of the other two.

"Please," said Mr. Sullivan kindly, "join us." They led the blackbirds to the center of our circle.

"A tribute to your poor departed mother," Uncle Seán announced. "May she rest in peace."

The blackbirds looked a little confused. But they just stood there, alone now in the middle of our circle. The music started up, and we started dancing. We kept our hands straight at our sides and kicked out our legs, one at a time, to the music. Kick, hop, kick, hop. Little by little, we moved toward the center, holding hands. Pretty soon we were shoulder to shoulder, like a kicking wall. Finally, I realized exactly what was going on. The three blackbirds couldn't get out of that circle if they tried.

the step dancers

All the people in the hall surrounded us, so there was wall after wall of people behind us dancers. Then Uncle Seán, Brendan, and Mrs. O'Malley moved in and broke through our ranks. By now, the three blackbirds looked petrified, I'll tell you!

Uncle Seán was carrying the yellow tin. Brendan had the photo of the real grave in Inishmore. Kate was holding the grave rubbing.

"What's going on?" demanded one of the thieves. All at once, the blackbirds tried to break out of the circle. Not a chance. The *gardaí* handcuffed them before they could go anywhere.

Uncle Seán held up the biscuit tin. "'Tis a pity you lost your pot of gold, Seamus!" he called as the *gardaí* led the head blackbird and his friends away.

"And 'tis a pity you tried to steal from the wrong people!" Mr. Sullivan added.

The thieves started mumbling and growling angrily, more like grizzly bears than blackbirds now.

"Thanks to the rest of you, our tin is overflowing!" Brendan shouted. "We begin construction tomorrow on the new Celtic Arts Centre!"

The crowd let out a huge cheer. You'd think they were a football team who'd just won the championship. (They call soccer "football" here in Ireland.) Everyone was whooping and cheering and stomping.

In the midst of all this, I thought I heard a

strange note whistling through one of the flutes, like wind. I listened. Yes. It was time. But it was too soon.

"Wait!" I yelled out loud to Lyra. "Let me stay one more day! I want to see castles with Molly, and ride a bike through the countryside, and…"

Too late! Before I knew it, I was whisked away.

Chapter 19

Peace at Last

Katie was still standing on her head, yoga-style, when I got back. David was still mad. I wasn't. For me, the whole silly argument was over.

"I'm sorry, David," I said. "I should have replaced your chess queen a long time ago."

Katie's feet landed on the floor with a *thud*.

"Well, that was easy!" she said. "I must be a good mediator!"

I glanced over at David. He looked suspicious.

"What happened to you?" he asked.

"I guess I had a sudden change of heart," I said.

"You had a sudden change of clothes, too!" said Katie. I looked down. I was still wearing my Irish dancing costume. Needless to say, it looked completely out of place.

"Oh, I...well..." I stammered. My gift of gab seemed to have temporarily vanished. I couldn't think of a good story to explain away my new fashion statement.

Quickly, to distract Katie and David, I dug into my backpack. There's usually something in there my angels have left me from the trip. This time, the pack was particularly heavy.

When I looked inside, my mouth dropped wide open. I pulled out a present for David.

"A peace offering," I said. I handed him a marble chess board, with a complete set of chess pieces.

David's present

"Queen and all!" I added. Then I ducked my head in my backpack so David couldn't hear me. "Thank you!" I whispered to whichever angel it was who had sent this home with me.

I've never seen David at such a loss for words. His face was filled with disbelief. "Why...? What...? Why didn't you give this to me before we got into that stupid fight?" he asked.

"Just set up the game," I told him.

Then I noticed something else in my backpack. I pulled it out while David was examining his new chess pieces, one at a time. It was an enormous red feather.

"What's that?" Katie asked, looking over my shoulder.

I had no idea. I supposed it was something I would need soon—for my next mission, maybe?

Katie snagged the feather from me and began fanning her face with it, in front of the mirror. It had a long quill on it, like a pen they had lettered the Book of Kells with. But the feather was definitely not from Ireland.

"This is real!" Katie said, handing it back. "It must have come from one huge bird!"

I stashed the feather carefully and turned back to David. He had the chess game all set up.

"Irish marble," he said, smiling in amazement. "I can't believe it, Hannah." He was so happy.

"Sure 'tis Connemara marble, to be exact," I said. "So are we friends again?"

"I'll think about it," David teased. But I knew everything was okay now.

I played with the loden and seafoam-green pieces. David played with the evergreen and pine. Of course, David won, as usual. But who cares? We were friends again.

And it was a great game.

Aran Islands—Three rocky islands in the Atlantic Ocean, west of Ireland. Molly and I were on the biggest island, Inishmore. The other two are Inishmaan and Inisheer. (Have you figured out yet that Inish means "island" in Gaelic?) They really do knit Aran sweaters here, and there really are no trees at all!

Black Fort—Ruins of a very old stone fort on the east cliffs of Inishmore. Its name in Gaelic is Dun Duchathair. (Try to pronounce *that!*) Part of this fort really did fall off into the ocean more than a hundred years ago.

Blarney Stone—Blarney Castle in County Cork, Ireland, has a special "magic" stone built into one of its walls. They say if you kiss the Blarney Stone (*Yuck!* How many people's lips have been there?), you're given the "gift of gab." There's a legend that says the castle was saved once because the people inside talked their way out of being attacked. (Clever, huh?)

Ceili—You say this word KAY-lee. It's an organized dance where people put on a show of traditional Irish dances like jigs, hornpipes, and reels. It also means a party where everybody gets together to dance.

Celtic—It's not pronounced SELL-tick, like the basketball team. You say it KELL-tick, like the *Book of Kells*. It refers to the Celts, who were early settlers in Ireland. They were very artistic and used beautiful curvy lines to decorate their jewelry, chariots, sculptures, and weapons (yes, artistic warriors!). The *Book of Kells* is one of the best examples of Celtic art. You can see it displayed at Trinity College in Dublin.

Firbolgs (fur-BULL-igs)—They're said to be pot-bellied creatures who can change their shape and become human if they want to.

Fungi—The name of a famous dolphin (kind of like Flipper) who lives in Dingle Bay, which is way south of the Aran Islands, in County Kerry.

Gaelic—The Irish language, which came from the Celts. Many people in the west of Ireland, especially in the Aran Islands, still speak Gaelic. The little mark used over some Gaelic words is called a *fada*. Seán's name has a *fada* over the "a."

Grave Rubbing—You can copy the words and pictures engraved on a gravestone by laying paper over it and rubbing it with a soft pencil or charcoal (or whatever else you happen to have in your backpack!).

Leprechauns (LEP-ruh-cons)—Those mischievous wee folk who like to play tricks on people who don't believe in them. If you are lucky enough to ever catch one, he has to give you his pot of gold!

Monastery—A place where monks live—no women, only men. In the fifth century (that was in the *four* hundreds!), the monks began to copy writings from Rome and Greece in beautiful lettering by hand. Later, monasteries were built by Irish monks all over Europe, where they kept copying important manuscripts. When the originals were lost, the monks had copies of them.

MUSICAL INSTRUMENTS

Concertina—Kind of like a small accordion.

Harp—You pluck the strings with your fingers to make angelic music!

Mandolin—An old-fashioned small string instrument you play like a guitar.

Penny Whistle—A thin, straight flute with a high-pitched "toot."

Recorder—Also a straight flute, but with a lower tone.

Nobel Peace Prize—A man named Alfred Nobel left a humongous amount of money in his will to be awarded to very special people who do great things for the world. Since 1901, prizes have been given for medicine and other sciences, literature, and peace.

Ogham—Sounds like "ome" in Irish (the "gh" is silent) and it's an old Celtic alphabet. Each letter is just a certain number of little marks drawn to the left or right of a long vertical line. You can still see it on some ancient standing stones in Ireland. It makes a great secret code. Here it is:

OGHAM

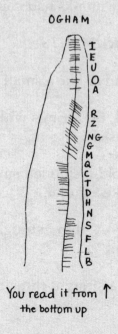

You read it from ↑
the bottom up

Peat Bog—An area of ground that's thick with water and mossy plant life. When peat is dried out, it can be used for fertilizer or for burning in a fireplace. (And my dad says no, I can't burn dirt from our garden. It doesn't have the same rich, organic stuff in it as the peat in Irish soil.)

Shamrock—A kind of green clover plant, usually with three little leaves. The shamrock is Ireland's national symbol. Finding one with four leaves is supposed to bring you good luck!

Soda Bread—*Mmmmm!* Great with butter and jam. It's made with baking powder instead of yeast, so you don't have to wait so long for the dough to rise. Every family has its own favorite recipe for soda bread: Some use wheat flour, some use white, and some people add raisins or currants.

Here's a sneak peek at

Hannah and the Angels #6
Mardi Gras Mix-up

Suddenly I heard the doorknob rattling. I turned in horror, as the door started to creak open.

A rush of panic went through me. Here I was, in a house where I didn't belong, in a room where I didn't belong, wearing a beautiful shawl that wasn't mine! I slipped the ticket into my skirt pocket and dashed to the other side of the bed, trying to scramble underneath to hide.

But it was too late. Just as my knees hit the floor, someone in a flowing glittery gown took a step in the door. It was a woman with beads and jewels dangling Gypsy-style from her neck and arms and ears. She had a deep-purple turban wrapped around her head, and long black finger-nails. And she was holding my red mask!

Slowly, from across the room, the woman pointed a long, bony finger right at my face...